"I bet you were all about curls and frills," Blake teased

He slowly pulled Maggie in closer. She didn't resist. Then, as if they'd done it a thousand times, he leaned in and gently kissed her neck, up and down each side, murmuring as he went. She felt a shiver race down her spine. "I was a tomboy…" She sighed, knowing she should stop this. She needed to stop this—she'd gotten too involved in his life already.

But she didn't.

He pulled back. "You?"

She nodded, grinning. "I've never admitted this to anyone, but my favorite pair of shoes were my cousin Emma's cowboy boots. They were two sizes too big. I wore them anyway."

He went back to kissing her neck, brushing her hair out of the way with his hands. A rush of heat played on her skin. Her body tingled.

"You're the most fascinating woman I've ever met," he said, merely brushing her lips with a kiss, tormenting her with his touch.

She pushed a few inches away from him, thinking she was going to end this, before they went any further. Instead she asked, "Are you going to kiss me on the mouth, or what?"

Dear Reader,

This is my first book for the Harlequin American Romance line, and I'm so excited to be with the series! What a treat to have found a new home. I've published with Harlequin before and had a great time writing those romances, but recently my heart has wandered into cowboy territory, and I'm so glad it did.

This love affair all began while I was attending a Zane Grey conference with some friends at Mormon Lake, Arizona. While there, I became fascinated with not only the works of Zane Grey, but with the mystique of the American cowboy. As the first evening wore on, and we were serenaded by old-time cowboy singers, I was introduced to Doc Miller, a real-life cowboy, pediatric dentist. He completely fascinated me with his fringed suede jacket, his dusty cowboy boots and hat, Wrangler jeans, a creamy tan-colored shirt and his absolute love of everything cowboy. He carried a cloth bag filled with kiddie toys and handed them out to everyone he met, including me. I chose a bright pink ring with a monster light-up plastic diamond, which I'm wearing right now…and did so while writing this book.

It wasn't long before Doc Blake was born, along with city girl, Maggie Daniels, and the fictional town of Briggs, Idaho.

I hope you enjoy reading this story as much as I enjoyed discovering it.

You can visit me at www.maryleo.net where I've posted a picture of my ring along with a few shots of the spectacular Teton Valley in Idaho.

Best,

Mary

Falling for the Cowboy

MARY LEO

HARLEQUIN®
entertain, enrich, inspire™

PLEASE RECYCLE · THIS PRODUCT IS RECYCLABLE

Recycling programs
for this product may
not exist in your area.

ISBN-13: 978-0-373-75427-4

FALLING FOR THE COWBOY

Copyright © 2012 by Mary Leo

www.Harlequin.com

Printed in U.S.A.

ABOUT THE AUTHOR

Mary Leo grew up in South Chicago in the tangle of a big Italian family. She's worked in Hollywood, Las Vegas and in Silicon Valley. Currently she lives in San Diego with her husband, author Terry Watkins, and their sweet kitty, Sophie.

For Catherine and Henry Nardi, who invited my husband and I to Zane Grey's West Society Annual Convention where I was introduced to Doc Miller (Doctor Stephen Miller), a pediatric cowboy dentist who is the inspiration for my character, Doc Blake. And for Terry Watkins, the love of my life, who buys me chocolate, makes me laugh and takes me on road trips.

To the incredibly supportive members of the RWASD Writing Challenge. I could have never written this book without you guys. You're simply the best!

Chapter One

Doctor Blake Granger, known to the locals as Doc Blake, the town's one and only pediatric dentist, took a monster bite out of a cake doughnut covered in sprinkles, then he closed his eyes for a moment, enjoying the complete bliss of early-morning sugar.

His sweet blitz had begun when he ordered a large coffee, black, and dumped in two packets of real sugar. He knew better than to mess around with refined sugar after having spent years warning his patients, "sugar rots your teeth." The statement rattled around the heads of most good dentists, but Blake was in an ornery mood this fine September morning and the mere idea of sugar—white, tooth-toxic sugar—seemed more important than his next breath.

He had snuck out of the main house at daybreak hoping to enjoy the crisp fall air, the fine dusting of snow that capped the Teton mountain range to the east of the ranch, and to slip off to Holey Rollers, the new doughnut shop, before anyone noticed he was gone.

So far, his plan seemed to be working.

Some of the pastel sprinkles clung to his mustache, while others trickled down his chin and settled on his flannel shirt. Earlier he'd knocked off two jelly doughnuts, a chocolate glazed twist and a mini cinnamon roll for good measure.

While he wiped away the evidence of his sugar fix with a paper napkin, he tried to remember the last time he'd indulged like this. Nothing came to mind. This kind of feather-headed behavior usually wasn't part of his makeup. His teeth were in grave peril, and if any of his patients saw him toying with the dark side of tooth decay they'd be throwing his own lectures back at him.

Fortunately, most of his patients preferred a Happy Meal to a cup of coffee and a doughnut.

Now he was sitting outside at one of the small ornate metal tables in front of the doughnut shop, enjoying his doughnut, a strong cup of coffee and the *Briggs Daily Journal,* another indulgence he rarely had time for, when an unfamiliar voice interrupted his revelry.

"Doctor Granger?"

"Yes, ma'am. That's me," he said, looking up at the face of a smiling woman standing next to his table.

Blake put his paper down and stood. The woman, dressed in a snug black business suit, was drop-dead gorgeous: long raven hair, crystal-blue eyes and a smile that could give a dying man reason to live.

She held out a hand, all businesslike, and for a moment Blake didn't know what to do. It was as if spring mud had flowed into his brain and covered all the working parts.

He hesitated, then came to his senses and took her hand in his. Just touching her sent a spark through his body. He wanted to pull back, but she had one of those professional tight-gripped handshakes, giving him no choice but to surrender to her touch.

"I'm Maggie Daniels, Kitty's sister."

She said it as if he already knew this, which he did not, and would never have guessed in a hundred years as he searched for a family resemblance.

Kitty was his pixie-cute office manager; she was getting ready to go out on early maternity leave due to twins. Of course, first she would be training her replacement, which she had already suggested could very well be her sister, Maggie, an idea that now made Blake uneasy. From a purely selfish point of view, he truly hoped his life wouldn't get any more complicated with the temporary changeover.

Between his willful father, the ranch, their looming potato harvest, his five-year-old daughter, his two brothers and almost-certain dental emergencies, Kitty's leave of absence could prove to be his undoing. She was his rock, and replacing her for even a few months seemed impossible.

"Great" was all he could manage to say.

Maggie finally let go of his hand, and Blake felt the mud clearing from his brain. "I mean, your sister's told me a lot about you."

She chuckled, then offered a flirty smile. "That could be dangerous."

He liked her sense of humor. "Only to your enemies."

"I already have enemies?"

"None so far."

"Give it time. It's a small town."

She had an edge to her that Blake wasn't quite sure how to take. No matter what he eventually decided to do about Kitty's replacement, he felt certain this woman would be a handful. "So, you're that kind of woman."

"What kind is that?"

"The kind that makes enemies."

"Only with other women. Men seem to like me."

He figured that was the case. "I come from a family of all boys."

"Then we shouldn't have a problem."

Reason told him Maggie was hell-bent for trouble. He was way over-the-moon attracted to her and he knew from experience what it meant to be attracted to a beautiful woman. His ex-wife was a beautiful woman and she had brought him nothing but grief. Maggie was even more of a threat with her haughty, big-city attitude, but damn it all, he was going to have a hard time saying no to her smile.

Not to mention that she had perfect teeth.

He gestured for Maggie to sit, and she pulled out the green metal chair across from him. The lady was all slicked up with a cream-colored blouse under her jacket that showed just the right amount of skin to make his mind wander to places it shouldn't be going. As she moved, he caught a glimpse of soft pink lace peeking out from under her blouse. It made him go all warm inside just knowing she wore girly pink under the tailored business suit that hugged her curves in all the right places.

Her face was flawless and her eyes reminded him of the early-morning sky on a cloudless day.

He picked up his coffee mug in an attempt to distract his wicked bedroom thoughts.

"I think you should know," she began, "that although I'm all for helping my sister, I have applications out to several other companies, and if one of them comes through, I might not be able to continue my employment with you for the duration of my sister's leave."

Blake took a long swig of his sweet coffee, thinking that he appreciated her honesty. "Not exactly what an employer wants to hear." He took another drink then carefully placed the white mug back on the table. "But who said I was going to hire you?"

She sat back and took up space, stretching out her long legs under the table and resting her arms on the chair. She seemed perfectly calm, totally cool and self-assured. "No one."

Blake eased down in his chair, sliding his Stetson low on his forehead, and pushing his legs out straight, crossing them at his ankles, only inches from her legs. He swore he could feel the heat of her, his legs getting all twitchy. What was it about this woman, that close proximity gave him an immediate physical reaction?

"How do I know you're qualified to run my office? It takes a special kind of person to work for me. What makes you think you're that person?"

"Confidence."

"In what?"

"Myself."

"Impressive, but can you tell me who Buzz Light-year's sidekick is in *Toy Story?*"

Maggie grinned at him, her amazing eyes sparkling with a bit of wickedness. He couldn't tell if she was trying to think of the answer or tickled that he'd asked such a childish question. Either way, Blake had her full attention.

Her smile revealed a slight dimple in her left cheek. He was a sucker for dimples, which made this little game they were playing even more perilous. He wanted to get to know her better—much better—but getting to know this kind of woman wasn't a tangle he needed to get caught up in ever again.

Still, there was something Country about her, something easy she kept hidden under all that city slicker show.

"Sheriff Woody. My favorite character, by the way."

He leaned in with the defining question, even though anyone listening would probably just laugh. Everything depended on her answer. "Do you own a pair of cowboy boots?"

"No…"

She looked hesitant.

Darn it all, he couldn't hire a woman who didn't own a pair of cowboy boots. They were a necessity in these parts, like a Leatherman tool or a trophy buckle. That fact alone proved she was just like his ex, and he didn't want or need a woman like her anywhere around him. Way too many bad memories of her disgust of everything Country.

"But my sister does, in an array of colors for some odd reason. We wear the same size, so in that sense, I'd have to amend my answer and say yes. I have access to cowboy boots. Why? Are they part of the job description?"

"I'd have to say they are."

She scooted up straight in her chair, crossing her fine legs under the table. "My sister never mentioned it."

He felt certain this was the stickler. "Huh. Can't figure why not. It's what we wear."

"Your office has a dress code?"

"Strictly enforced." Not exactly true, but now he was desperate.

"Anything else I should know about?"

His mind raced to think of something, anything, that this temptation in heels might not like, but mud had once again settled in parts of his head and he couldn't seem to come up with a thing.

He knew he could save himself a whole lotta grief if he simply hired Mrs. Abernathy, the seventy-year-old ex-nurse who had offered to take the job. Unfortunately, Kitty had already warned him not to do it. Mrs. Abernathy was inflexible in her ways and tone deaf. No way could she sing to his patients or run the office the way Kitty had set it up.

He wondered if Maggie could hold a tune. "We sometimes have to sing to the patients."

"I don't sing. Completely tone deaf."

Her answer was his out. His escape hatch. His *adios, amigo.* Even Kitty would agree on this one.

Maggie stared at him, looking all pretty in the morning sun, and Blake had to admit a part of him wanted nothing more than to have her around for the next fifty years. But the danger of falling for someone so like his ex-wife meant grabbing the branding iron by the hot end, and he was not in the mood for another round of hurt.

Blake stalled for a time, pretending he was chewing on her answer, while he screwed up his flailing courage.

He had thought moving back to the family ranch in eastern Idaho with his dad and brothers would have slowed his life down, especially after living in L.A. for several years, but it had been nothing like that. When

Blake had arrived in Briggs, he'd hit the ground running, and he'd been going nonstop ever since. Maggie Daniels was the kind of woman who would only tangle up his spurs, and at this point, he wasn't sure he was up for the challenge.

Just then his phone chimed. "Excuse me," he said. The phone's screen illuminated the name Lindsey Luntz. Her thirteen-year-old son, Chad, was a patient of Blake's. Chad was having difficulty adjusting to his new braces and he probably needed a "cheer up, buckaroo" talk, which would take some time, knowing Chad. Blake took the call, but asked Mrs. Luntz to hold.

"I have to take this," he told Maggie. Then, as though he didn't have anything under his hat but hair, he said, "See you in the morning. Eight-thirty?"

She nodded.

"Kitty can tell you the rest."

"Thanks," she said.

Feeling muddy-headed again, he tried to get his wits honed back to concentrate on the waiting Mrs. Luntz.

Blake watched as Maggie pushed herself up from the chair, gave him a little smile, turned and walked away.

He stared after her as she sashayed into the doughnut shop. The woman had one of those walks that made a man stare—hips gently swaying, elegant legs careful of each step in her fancy high heels, straight back and hair that glistened in the sunlight. Desire swept through him.

His breath caught in his throat and he found it difficult to wrest his gaze from Maggie until he heard Mrs. Luntz calling his name. "Doc Blake? Are you there? Doctor? Darn these phones."

MAGGIE WALKED INTO Holey Rollers and ordered a double cappuccino, dry, and a blueberry muffin. She wanted something decadent with sprinkles to celebrate the occasion, but her hips didn't need it. Once she'd turned thirty, everything she ate seemed to stick to her hips.

Despite that misfortune, Maggie knew she still had it, could still turn a man's head when she wanted to. The good doctor had proven that. She had seen the attraction in his eyes. Heard it in his voice.

Sure, she had other job applications out, but the likelihood of any of them coming through was remote. Still, she felt she had to tell him the truth and rely on her looks to get him to hire her anyway.

Maggie couldn't hide the fact that the overly judgmental world labeled her as beautiful. She didn't dwell on it, rather, it was a truth she had come to accept. Still, more than anything, she had always wanted to be treated like a normal girl—a buddy other women could confide in, or a girlfriend to some sweet guy who loved to cuddle on the sofa, eat popcorn drenched in real butter and watch old movies.

Regrettably, she had little experience with any of those things.

Ever since she could remember, she had been the outcast in any group of girls, the cufflink on the man with power and the catch for the guy who wanted to elevate his social status.

Her only friend—her only confidant and ally— during all of the insanity of her life was her sister, Kitty.

Maggie thought Kitty was amazingly beautiful, more beautiful than Maggie could ever be. Apparently, the world hadn't caught on to that fact. And because of the oversight, Kitty had led a relatively ordinary life. A life Maggie hungered to call her own, especially after her latest breakup with Brad Allen, the lying, cheating dog of a man who'd had the nerve to propose to her while he was sleeping with his secretary.

Once Maggie caught them, she was out of the relationship and out of the job she loved. She had worked hard to become vice president of marketing for Silicon Systems, but there was no way she could stay after she'd learned the truth. Brad was executive V.P. of the entire company. No getting around the scandal.

So, after nearly four months of unanswered resumes, she finally had a job, albeit a temp job in a town so small it had taken three drive-bys just to find the right exit. It was a paycheck nonetheless.

The girl behind the counter turned to Maggie. "That'll be three dollars and sixty-five cents." Her name tag read Amanda. She wore her mahogany hair extra-short, which accentuated her bright red lipstick and dangly earrings. Maggie guessed that Amanda was closing in on eighteen.

Maggie leaned in across the counter, certain that Amanda must have forgotten to ring up one of her items. "That was a double cappuccino and a muffin."

Amanda rolled her eyes and leaned in closer, as if she didn't want anyone else to hear. "I know. Like, my boss raised the price on some of the pastries last week, thinking nobody would notice. I told her people were going to complain, but, like, did she listen? Noo. Nobody ever listens to me. I bet you never get that, especially wearing that suit, huh?"

Maggie smiled, noticed everyone clad in casual

clothing and felt completely out of place. The tiny shop was crowded with customers hovering in front of the glass doughnut counter, desperately trying to make up their minds while three other employees in light brown aprons with the Holey Rollers logo emblazoned across their chests, eagerly waited to fill their sugar fix. An assortment of doughnuts, muffins and other pastries, all of which looked incredible, filled every inch of the glass display, with the extras stacked on metal baking shelves along the walls. The shop smelled sweet, with just the right amount of freshly brewed coffee scent wafting through the air.

"I had a job interview."

"With Doc Blake?"

"You mean Doctor Granger?"

"Everyone calls him Doc Blake. It's easier."

Maggie liked the nickname. It fit him. "Yes."

Amanda gazed out the front window at the doctor. She let out a heavy sigh. "Like, I've had a crush on him ever since he pulled out my wisdom teeth. I think every girl in this town's got a thing for Doc Blake. I'd give anything if he was mine, but ever since that low-life, Bethany Walker, broke his heart he won't even look at another girl. And, like, believe me, plenty of us have tried, but it's like his heart's been broken in too many pieces. Sort of like that old kid's rhyme, Humpty Dumpty. Shame. I'd be perfect for him." She sighed again, while staring out at Doc Blake, but quickly turned back to Maggie. "So, like, you must be Kitty's sister?"

Maggie wondered how this girl would know that. After all, this was a coffee and doughnut shop. Two things her sister forbade in her all-organic-all-the-time, eco-friendly house. "You know my sister?"

Amanda cocked her head and rolled her eyes, reminding Maggie of the size of the town. "Large organic chocolate soy, with extra whipped cream. Comes in at least three times a week. She told me you were driving up and might take over her job for a while. Kitty's, like, the best."

"Does she ever order anything else?" Maggie had to know if her sister was a closet doughnut eater.

"She looks, and sometimes if we put some pieces out for tasting, she'll snitch one, but no, just the chocolate soy. Personally, like, when I get pregnant? I intend to eat everything I want. It's like the only time a woman can indulge without feeling guilty."

"I'll have to remember that."

"Why, are you pregnant, too?"

Maggie blanched. "Me? Pregnant? Absolutely not." Amanda stared at her. Maggie got the feeling that not wanting children was an unpopular idea in this town. She thought she should clarify. "I'm not very good with kids. An aunt is about as close as I'll ever come to having kids of my own."

Amanda blinked a couple times, bagged the muffin and handed it to Maggie. "You're going to come a lot closer than that working for Doc Blake, that's for sure." And she walked away.

The barista called Maggie's name for her double cap, yet Maggie didn't move. Instead, she wanted to know what Amanda had meant by that last statement. She tried to get her attention, but there were now so many customers it seemed impossible.

There was something up with Doctor Blake Granger

that Kitty hadn't told her, but what? She knew he was a dentist who worked out of an office on his ranch, but that was about all Kitty had told her. What was the kid connection and how could it affect Maggie?

It wasn't as if Maggie didn't already have her doubts about working for Doc Blake. For one thing, she didn't exactly love the idea of working around all those high-pitched drills. Truth be told, a visit to the dentist had always put the fear of God in her, but she needed a job and Kitty needed some help, so giving in to her drill fear was not an option.

Hey, all of this was temporary, she reminded herself. Of that she was absolutely certain.

Her sister may have found her niche, her own personal Idaho nirvana, but Maggie belonged to the city, with concrete and skyscrapers—not mountains, as lovely as they were—surrounding her.

She picked up her coffee, then stopped near the glass-front door and took a sip of her double cappuccino. Heaven. She slipped the plastic lid off and breathed in the smooth aroma of real, honest-to-goodness espresso. It was truly an intoxicating experience and she stood next to the condiment stand in front of the windows for a minute to enjoy the moment. Having been deprived of actual coffee for the past few days due to her sister's coffee restrictions, Maggie wanted nothing more than to wallow.

Before she walked to her car, and while Doc Blake was totally distracted by his phone call, Maggie glanced through the window at him to see what all the fuss was about. She hadn't actually seen anything special about him during the interview, but then she'd been a bit nervous about meeting him and convincing him to hire her. Focusing on his charms hadn't seemed worthwhile.

The first thing she now noticed, besides those deep dark eyes of his, and the blond hair that ambled down his neck covering his collar and that sexy mustache, were the well-worn cowboy boots under his frayed jeans, not to mention the chocolate-colored felt cowboy hat he wore low on his head.

He seemed to be in his mid-thirties, and she began to see why half the women in the town had a crush on him. He was all rugged country charisma under that old hat, with a smile that could easily send a naive girl's heart soaring.

"He sure is something to look at, isn't he?" An older woman sighed as she came up to Maggie clutching a white dish towel. She wore the same logo apron as the rest of the staff, and her name tag read Doris.

"Very handsome," Maggie admitted while Doris wiped down the kiosk.

"Wish I was twenty years younger," Doris cooed, staring out the window at Doc Blake.

But Maggie had had her fill of good-looking, charming men. They pulled out that sympathy card and women threw themselves at their feet. There was nothing like a wounded hero to get an otherwise sensible woman into his bed.

Not this time. And most definitely not in this small town.

Downtown Briggs consisted of exactly three blocks of attached brick buildings with glass storefronts. The majestic Teton mountain range was its backdrop. It could be quite a spectacular place, if it wasn't for the corniness of some of the shops.

Maggie couldn't imagine settling in a town that allowed a huge plaster potato to be perched on the roof of the Spud Bank directly across the street from Holey Rollers, or the monster plaster llama that stood watch in front of Deli Llama's. But her favorite was the black-and-white life-sized cow standing in front of Moo's Creamery, complete with pink udders. She wondered if the entire business community was caught up in some kind of silly name contest and these were the big winners. Part of her thought they were cute, while the city girl in her thought they should be outlawed.

"Look, Doc's leaving," Doris announced as if the sun had just dropped from the sky.

Maggie's attention fell back on Doctor Granger. He was laughing now as he stood up, a tall, slim man with a muscular build. And when two elderly ladies pushed open the door to the doughnut shop, she could hear his great big baritone guffaw. She liked a man who could laugh like that. Most guys in the business community seemed to be too nervous to really laugh. To let it rip. She'd almost forgotten what that kind of male laughter sounded like. For some reason it made her feel happy and safe…or maybe it was the coffee. She couldn't be sure.

All she really knew at the moment was that Doc Blake drank real coffee, ate real sugar and had a fabulous laugh. Maybe it wouldn't be so bad working for him and living in this colorful town while Kitty was on maternity leave. At least she could collect a paycheck until something more permanent came along.

This time, Maggie would sit back and watch all the other women swoon over her heartbroken boss.

Maggie thankfully wasn't the least bit interested in a relationship. And according to Amanda, neither was the good doctor.

Chapter Two

"This is going to work out so perfectly that I feel calm already," Kitty told Maggie. "I knew it would. I dropped off a thank-you basket of goodies at the ranch about an hour ago."

Maggie could only imagine what that completely organic basket contained, something raw or dried or juiced no doubt.

They were standing in Kitty's overly bright and cheerful kitchen, completely created with vintage linens, salvaged wood and reclaimed natural materials. Lovely as everything was, Maggie longed for the familiarity of laminated flooring and labels like Ikea, Williams-Sonoma and Crate & Barrel.

"I wouldn't say we hit it off. It was more that we can probably work together effectively."

"He's the easiest boss ever. You're going to love working for him." Kitty peeled the top off a pint-sized plain Greek-style yogurt, sat down at the table and dug in.

"How can you eat that stuff? Don't you miss the fruit and sugar?"

"Refined sugar is the enemy. It's responsible for a litany of bodily ailments, including heart disease."

"Yeah, but it tastes sweet."

"So does radiator coolant."

Maggie looked at her, puzzled. "How do you know these things?"

"My sweet hubby's parents own a hardware store over in Idaho Falls. Nice town, but a little too big for us."

"Unless they drink the stuff for breakfast, how would they know that?"

Kitty shrugged. "They just do."

"Oh, okay then. Sugar is off the table. Is honey acceptable?"

Kitty hesitated, as if making up her mind. "It's stressful to the bees."

"Isn't that their job?"

"Not all jobs are good for you."

Maggie stared at Kitty then blinked a couple times. Ever since she'd moved in a week ago, she had learned how to create her own kitchen compost, how to recycle effectively, and more recently, how to bake the perfect flourless cake using some kind of cactus sugar. A dessert Maggie would never be fully able to appreciate.

"We can't have this conversation."

"Okay," Kitty said, then made a couple of yummy sounds. She took another big bite of the yogurt and put the spoon down on the table, resting her hands on her belly as a smile stretched across her sweet face. "Thank you again for doing this. Except for a couple of Tim's cousins, and an obstinate great-aunt who pops in whenever she sees fit, and the occasional visit from Tim's parents—I couldn't ask for more supportive in-laws, but with their store hitting some rough times, it's hard for them to leave it—I'm kind of on my own here. Not that I mind. We chose to live in Briggs, and I love it. I've made a lot of friends here, but family is different."

Kitty looked radiant, and seemed happy to have Maggie living with her. For that, Maggie was willing to endure just about anything.

"Don't be silly. You saved me. My unemployment checks were barely making it, and I had no idea how much longer I was going to be able to keep my car. Plus, searching for a job in Silicon Valley was getting me nowhere. If I were Allison Bennett, the absolute goddess of marketing, I'd have twenty job offers by now, but I'm Maggie Daniels. Nobody cares."

"I care, and you're a fantastic marketing, social media guru. People will be knocking down your door. They just don't know you're free, that's all. When the right person finds out, he or she will come calling. You wait and see."

Maggie loved her sister's enthusiasm, but no one had come knocking so far, and they clearly wouldn't come knocking in this remote potato town.

"Country life is a nice change. But I have to admit, working in a dental office five days a week, and being that close to all those nasty little drills, may put me over the edge. You know how much I hate having my own teeth worked on."

"That's not what's bugging you. Not really. I think you're upset because you think it's an insignificant job with no future and that your baby sister should be soaring up the ladder, like you, instead of stuck on a broken lower rung." Kitty's eyes welled up. "You just don't get it. I'm not that corporate person anymore."

"Why are you crying? I would never think any less of you or your choices."

"You're my sister. You're supposed to say that. I love you, and—" She paused and took a few ragged breaths before continuing. "I'm pregnant, and my husband is a million miles away and I miss him."

The woman would cry or rage at least twice a day. Maggie didn't know how Tim, her husband, would ever have been able to deal with it. Although, Tim was one of those rare men who actually loved everything about his wife. It seemed that anything Kitty did or said, especially during her pregnancy, was just short of perfection.

But he wasn't around every day to enjoy all her hormonal moments. Captain Tim Sullivan was busy on the other side of the world, fighting a war.

Maggie went over to her. She hated to see Kitty cry. And even if what she said was true, Kitty was still her baby sister and Maggie would do anything for her baby sister, including giving up honey because it stressed the bees. "It's okay, sweetie. Don't cry. Actually, I'm thinking this is a great opportunity for me to make your life a little easier while we wait for those two sweethearts to be born. I'm happy things have happened this way or I would never have been able to spend this much time with you." Maggie leaned over and gave Kitty a tight hug. "It was my nerves talking. Clearly, I'm thrilled to have a job. It's just that I'm apprehensive of the actual duties. I don't have any real experience that relates. You know how I like being prepared."

Kitty gently pulled away, drying her eyes on the white hankie she always kept in a pocket for just such an occasion.

"Really?"

Maggie nodded, giving Kitty her warmest smile,

thinking that her little sister really was quite beautiful, even with a tear-streaked face. Pregnancy agreed with her.

"Thanks," Kitty said, getting comfy on the wooden chair, her round belly pushing up against the table. "Don't you go worrying about a thing. I'll go in with you all week until you get the hang of it. There are no insurance forms, or a paper trail of any kind. Everything is done on the computer." Kitty ate a couple of big scoops of yogurt and continued. "I'm telling you, this will be the easiest bull you'll ever ride. Everybody loves Doc Blake. He's the best in the West."

Ever since her sister had moved to Idaho three years ago, her language had taken on an odd country flair. Not that it was bad, but it was certainly different.

"It's really a fun office. You'll see," Kitty said.

Maggie flashed on what Amanda from the doughnut shop had said, about how she was going to get closer to kids or something like that. She had been determined to ask Kitty what that might mean, but at the moment, she didn't want to upset her again. Any little thing could turn on the waterworks and Maggie simply didn't want to go there.

Instead, she thought she'd gently find out some information. She poured herself a glass of local spring water and sat across from Kitty at the table.

"I was just wondering what, if anything, you might have told Doctor Granger, or Doc Blake as everyone seems to call him, about me?"

"Well, I knew what a pickle you were in, but if you mean did I tell him you were dating a slug who pretended to be in love with you, when, in fact, he was bonking his secretary who turned out to be a crazy woman who most likely keyed your new BMW, punched out your headlights, was responsible for your losing your six-figure position and is most likely responsible for your willingness to come to Briggs, Idaho, for a job that you're completely overqualified for? No. I didn't tell him."

Maggie let out the breath she'd been holding. She so didn't want anyone in this thimble of a town to know about her sordid past. It was embarrassing enough that most of her friends had abandoned her over the whole ordeal. She clearly didn't need her new boss whispering behind her back. Not that he seemed the type, but she couldn't be sure of anything anymore.

"Thanks."

"I'm your sister, remember? I'm on your side."

Now Maggie felt like crying. The whole miserable affair with her ex-fiancé was still raw, and talking about it ripped the scab off the wound.

"And you can forget about Doc Blake as a rebound lover," Kitty added, scraping the container for the last bites of yogurt. "He's a died-in-the-wool Briggs resident and wouldn't leave again if his life depended on it. You'd have to move in permanent-like if you two got together."

"Relax. I have no intention of anything close to 'permanent-like' in Briggs. I don't intend to date anyone while I'm here, especially not my boss. No offense to you or any of the other women in this town, but I just don't get what all the fuss is about. Yeah, he's cute, in that country sort of way, but I'm a rock and roll kind of girl. Coldplay, U2 and Daughtry turn me on, not George Jones."

"We'll see. This town grows on you."

"Maybe on you, little sister, but never on me."

Kitty smirked as she polished off the yogurt and pushed the empty container aside. "*Never* is greatly overrated. I'm just sayin'."

"Always the optimist."

"It's all about what messages we send out into the universe. If we're positive, positivity comes back to us, whereas if we're negative...." She raised an eyebrow.

"I'm a realist. I know who I am."

"Maybe, but I'm just sayin'."

BY THE TIME Blake pulled his mud-encrusted pickup in front of the family ranch house, the sky had turned a brilliant mix of pink, gold and deep blue against the backdrop of the black mountains. The golden aspens that surrounded this old log house were rustling in the warm breeze reminding him of why he had returned to Idaho. This was his favorite time of year, and he was grateful he wasn't back in L.A., stuck on a freeway.

It didn't matter that his day had been consumed with patients. Looking out over this spectacular piece of land nestled in the Teton Valley, Blake knew leaving Los Angeles had been the right decision.

It had been a long day that started off with caffeine, doughnuts and Maggie Daniels. Both the doughnuts and Maggie Daniels were bad for him, but he didn't seem to care. Maggie was stuck in his head just as sure as come tomorrow morning he'd be stopping by Holey Rollers for a repeat performance.

Maggie had been jumbled up in his thoughts all day. She'd been there while he was giving Chad a pep talk about how great his teeth would look once the braces were off, and how all smart cowboys had their teeth straightened. She was there as he shared coffee with Chad's mom, Lindsey, giving her advice on how to handle Chad's situation in the future.

He had thought of her as he descended Lindsey's front steps and spoke on his cell to Jimmy Ferguson's mom, who was requesting an emergency extraction for young Jimmy's loose front tooth. His mom couldn't possibly inflict pain of any kind on her son, so it was up to Blake to do the deed.

Back in his office, the tooth slid out with barely a budge. Young Jimmy was so into watching *Toy Story 3* on the ceiling monitor that he hadn't noticed his tooth had been extracted.

Blake gave him the offending tooth in a tiny brown pouch so the tooth fairy could bring him a present in the morning. "I want to go home, home, home, Mommy," Jimmy said. "I need to put this under my pillow right away, just in case the tooth fairy buzzes our house looking for bags of teeth. I don't want her to miss mine."

His mom agreed and off they went.

Blake loved the fact that he had patients young enough to believe in tooth fairies and Santa. Kids were easy. Adults were the kicker.

When that was over and he cleaned up, once again his thoughts drifted to Maggie and that salty walk of hers. Then, just as he was getting into a cozy fantasy about her, his phone rang and he agreed to drive over to Angie Barnett's house. Angie was a first-time mom with a teething baby girl, who was desperate for some sleep.

After he checked out her screaming tot, he told Angie, "My mom would dip her pinky in whiskey, shake off the excess and rub it on her babies' swollen gums. But some moms don't like the idea of alcohol touching their baby, so it's up to you."

The baby let out an ear-piercing scream and Angie didn't hesitate to rub the child's gums with brandy.

"Please, oh, please," Angie said as her baby chomped on her fingers, and within minutes the baby was as calm as a cat in the sun.

Blake gave Angie a few rubber teething toys he kept in an emergency kit in his pickup, and the combination seemed to work miracles.

By the time he eventually left, both Angie and her baby were fast asleep.

Another laid-back Sunday.

For once, he'd like to spend an entire Sunday doing nothing of any importance. Not that he didn't enjoy helping his patients, but the thought of an entire day off seemed almost as impossible as trying to trim the whiskers off the man in the moon.

He climbed the wooden porch stairs of his ranch house and was greeted by Suzy and Mush. He bent over to give both dogs some good lovin'. They were siblings, part wolf with a whole lot more parts mutt. It was the mutt parts that loved attention and the wolf parts that kept critters out of the house and barn.

Wrestling with the dogs reminded him that Maggie Daniels had consumed him the entire day, even while he was singing "Home on the Range" to Angie's baby.

For some reason, he couldn't get rid of her image—those long legs, the girly underwear, and that sparkle in her eyes—but that didn't mean he wanted her there with him. Regrettably, he had almost no control over his subconscious, where she now lived as sure as he knew he was dog-tired and wanted nothing more than to sit down with his family and share Sunday dinner, a perfectly cooked rib roast. Blake anticipated that first scrumptious bite as he grabbed the doorknob and swung open the front door, Suzy and Mush following close behind.

No matter what else happened during the week, come six o'clock on Sunday night it was dinner with the family. He could count on it like prairie flowers in spring.

"Daddy's home," his five-year-old daughter, Scout, shouted as soon as she spotted him. She came running toward him at full throttle, arms outstretched, ready to grab hold and give him her tightest squeeze. Her miniature cowboy boots were clacking across the wooden floor, strawberry-colored hair in its usual state of disarray, blue shirt falling out of her britches, and a look of absolute love on her adorable face.

For the umpteenth time since they had moved back to Briggs, Blake fully realized that his sweet daughter desperately needed what all the kids he'd treated that day already had: a loving mom. Unconditional and all-consuming love was an emotion Scout's own mom sorely lacked.

Living in a house filled with boys had turned his little girl into a blustering tomboy. So much so that she had wanted to cut off all her hair—something Blake was not ready to accept. Not that he thought there was anything wrong with those tough-boy traits, but he wondered if Scout missed pink and had settled for blue to fit in with the rest of the family. But most of all he wondered just how much she missed the fuss and love a woman could give her. He knew it was time he found someone else to share his life with, but so far, he'd been too busy. Maybe he needed to do something about that.

He whisked his child up in his arms and twirled her around. They eventually landed on the sofa with his younger brother Colt's three boys getting in on the fun, along with Suzy, who loved a good tussle. Mush sat on his haunches and barked.

Colt's boys ranged in age from three to six, and all were loved like crazy by their father and the rest of the men in the Granger family. The boys' mother had passed away from complications right after giving birth to the youngest, Joey. Colt never faltered in his dedication to his boys, especially to Joey.

"Dinner's sittin' on the table," Blake's father, Dodge, announced. He was a tall man, six foot four, with a stride like John Wayne, and a temperament like molasses. Nothing fazed him, ever, and in the scheme of Blake's chaotic life, his dad's rock-solid demeanor was the anchor that kept him grounded.

Dodge ran the house, cooked most of the meals and essentially kept the place from falling completely apart, especially during potato harvest season, which was coming up in a few weeks. This was where Dodge and Colt had it all over Blake. They ran the agricultural part of the ranch while Travis, his youngest brother, took care of the livestock. Blake contributed his time when he could, but essentially he had his hands full with his dental practice.

Blake had wanted to be a pediatric dentist ever since he'd been thrown from a horse when he was twelve and dislodged his two front teeth on a rock. Everyone thought he would lose those teeth, but Doc Greeley saved them with his expertise. Blake thought it was cool and became friends with the doctor who was soon his mentor. Colt and Travis gave him a rash about his obsession with teeth for the longest time, and when it came time for Blake to go off to college or get serious about ranching, he chose UCLA School of Dentistry in Los Angeles. Then when Doc Greeley retired and moved away right around the time Blake and Scout moved back to Briggs, he took over Doc's practice, a dream he'd had ever since he was a boy.

The kids raced to the table to take their seats. Dodge sat at one end and Blake sat at the other. Travis and Colt sat one on either side in between the kids, acting as wranglers.

The table was set with the same mustard-colored, Fiestaware plates that had been a tradition in the family ever since Blake's mom was alive. She had liked everything to be neat and color-coordinated just like in a magazine. Unfortunately, she had a house filled with boys, so nothing was ever quite up to her satisfaction.

A large bowl of Idaho mashed spuds sent up steam on one end of the wooden table along with a platter of mixed grilled veggies and a large wooden bowl filled with salad. Simple, but satisfying. A loaf of freshly baked rosemary bread from On The Rise bakery sat on a cutting board ready to be sliced. The two dogs made themselves comfortable under the table near Dodge.

"So," Travis began once a short prayer of thanks had been said and the side dishes began to make their way around the table. "Amanda, over at Holey Rollers, said Kitty's sister was checking you out through the window this morning. What's up with that? Has yet another woman fallen for the poor, suffering Doc Blake?"

"Oh, Daddy, did you eat a doughnut?" Scout wanted to know.

Blake had no choice but to come clean. "Yes, I did." He was not about to tell her how many.

Colt said, "I hear she's hotter than a burnt boot. Just your type, big brother. Too much woman wrapped up in a city suit."

"You were bad, Daddy. They'll rot your teeth."

"Yeah, Uncle Blake, sugar is the enemy," Colt's oldest, Buddy, chimed in.

"I'm not interested in Kitty's sister," Blake told Colt, but he knew he didn't say it with much conviction.

"Busted," Joey announced while holding up his fork.

"Out of the mouths of babes," Travis joked.

Blake held up a hand. "Wait a minute." He turned to Scout. "I brushed when I got into the office, like any good cowboy should."

Colt pressed on. "Amanda said you interviewed the sister to take Kitty's place when she leaves."

Blake wished everyone would get off his case, but he was used to taking a ribbing from his brothers. They'd been digging into him ever since they learned to put two words together.

Travis added, "From the sound of it, seems like she wants more from you than just a job."

Colt doled out salad for himself and his two boys. Dodge rose, muttering about forgetting the main dish, and headed for the kitchen. "You're not seriously thinking of hiring her, are you? Sounds like a carbon copy of the last woman who got under your skin. And we all know how that went down."

Blake wanted to tell everyone to back off. That he had it all under control. That he wouldn't hire Maggie. But the truth was he'd already hired her, and if he didn't stop himself he was certain to head down the same dismal road, just like Colt warned.

Darn it all, he hated when his brothers were right.

Dodge reappeared, carrying what looked like a baked turkey roll on a white platter.

Blake immediately felt cheated. "What's that?"

"Somethin' called tofurkey," Dodge said. "Made with some of that extra-firm type tofu, a little herb stuffin', some mushrooms and a whole bunch'a celery. It's a gift from Kitty who whipped it up herself, thankin' us 'cause Blake here hired her sister, Maggie."

"Here we go again," Travis said, as he shook his head.

Blake decided to ignore Travis and focus on their poor excuse for a rib-eye roast. "Come on, Dad. You can't be serious." He was starving, but he'd rather eat his own boot than one of Kitty's *healthy* creations.

"Kitty was good enough to go to all the trouble of makin' it and luggin' it over here, especially in her female condition. We got no choice but to eat it. We don't waste no food in this house."

"Does it have peanuts in it? I like peanuts," Joey asked.

"Most likely," Blake answered.

"Can't we give it to people who like health food?" Gavin, Colt's middle son, asked.

"This here's a small town, son," Dodge explained. "Kitty would hear about it before the first bite was taken, and that would hurt her feelin's. You don't want to be puttin' a hurt on Kitty, now do you, son? No tellin' what that woman might do."

Gavin shook his head in resignation.

Dodge began slicing the tofurkey then plating it for his family. Joey was the only one at the table who seemed eager to eat his dinner. Everyone else wore a combination of fear and disgust on their faces. Blake was especially not eager to try it.

"Is Kitty going away, Daddy? I don't want Kitty to go away. She's my friend. I don't want you to hire the hot boot lady. I want Kitty." Big tears rolled down Scout's cheeks.

Blake immediately stood and went over to her. He had a feeling the tears might be about something— someone—else. He knelt down beside his child as she tumbled into his arms. "Hey, baby, Kitty's not going away. Not like you think she is. Kitty has to take some time off to have her babies. Once they're born and she's rested a bit, she'll come right back to the office here. I promise."

When the tears intensified, he carried Scout out to the front porch with Suzy following close behind. Wherever Scout went on the ranch, Suzy was usually right there with her.

Blake sat on the swing, placing Scout next to him. The sun had set, and the world around them was growing dark. Birds busied themselves up in the trees with a rush of evening song while Blake gently rocked the swing back and forth. A whitetail buck lazily grazed about twenty feet from the house, as if it knew he was safe from hunters on the Granger ranch.

The combination of movement, watching the buck and bird chatter seemed to calm Scout, though it took a few minutes before she stopped crying. When she finally caught her breath, she said, "She won't ever come back, Daddy, and I'll miss her too much. I don't want her to go. Make her stay."

Blake sat back as his daughter reached up, wrapped her arms around his neck and started crying again. He stroked her hair, and leaned into her. "Kitty isn't going anywhere, baby. She's staying home for a while, that's all. You can visit her anytime you want."

Scout sat back down and wiped her eyes with the back of her hands. "She's not moving to L.A.?"

"Whatever gave you that idea?"

"Mommy moved to L.A."

"We all did, sweetpea, but we came back."

"But Mommy didn't. I want her to come home now."

Blake's heart was breaking. "That's not possible, baby. Her job is in L.A."

"Can't she move her job here?"

"I'm afraid not, but how about if I call her right now so you can talk to her?"

She nodded. "Okay."

Scout slid over on the swing, getting closer to him, waiting.

As Blake pulled his phone out to make the call, he knew before Maggie Daniels set one foot inside his office, he'd have to fire her. No matter what he thought of Maggie, he knew his brothers were right. She would prove to be exactly like his ex, who, once again, was screening her calls and would call him back later, when she knew Scout would be in bed.

Chapter Three

"I'm really tired," Kitty announced as she dumped dry black beans into a pot to soak overnight, no doubt for some tasty new cake recipe she'd discovered in her latest vegan cookbook.

"Then you should go to bed," Maggie told her. "I can take care of cleaning up."

"But it's only seven o'clock, and I wanted to finish knitting those booties for my babies."

"You can knit tomorrow. Your babies aren't due for at least another five weeks. You have plenty of time."

Kitty yawned, then said, "You're right." And she waddled off in the direction of her bedroom with Maggie following close behind.

Once Kitty was comfortably tucked into bed, with pillows scrunched under her legs, arms and head, Maggie kissed her forehead and turned out the lights. Then, she walked to her room down the hall, changed into tight-fitting jeans, combed her hair out so it hung loose on her shoulders, reapplied her makeup a little darker than she had worn it during the day and sprayed on her favorite perfume.

Tonight, Maggie was going out. She finally had a reason to celebrate, and she refused to do it with a glass of organic sparkling cider. She hadn't been able to justify a night out for quite a while, but now that she had a job, a glass of red wine seemed in order, along with the fattest steak her money could buy.

Normally, only her platform stilettos would do with her skinny jeans, but she needed to start fitting in if she was going to live in this tumbleweed of a town for the next few months, so cowboy boots seemed to be the ticket.

After quietly trying on several pairs of her sister's boots, she settled on a slightly worn burnt-orange pair with a respectable heel, and a subtle pointed toe. She borrowed a deep blue sweater, and wrapped a white wool scarf around her neck. She went back to her own room and slid two crisp twenty-dollar bills into her back pocket and headed out for Belly Up, the bar she'd seen a few blocks away.

As soon as she opened Belly Up's heavy glass door, country music bounced from every hard surface causing the floor to vibrate with its steady beat. She knew she was stepping into a real honky-tonk complete with bare wooden planks on the floor, and a mirrored mahogany bar that extended along the entire west wall.

A rather large painting of a nude, round woman with a thin draping of white fabric across her privates, lounging on a bright-pink velvet chaise, hung on the far wall behind a group of tables occupied by patrons eating dinner. The smell of beer dominated the air and caused Maggie to wonder if the place even served anything but a cold one.

She hesitated in the open doorway, not quite sure if she was up to a hardcore-Country night out in Briggs, Idaho. Thinking how different all this was from her favorite martini bar in Pacific Heights in San Francisco, for a moment she considered leaving. Sparkling cider wasn't all that bad, especially if she pretended it was sweet champagne.

"Nice boots," a man's voice said behind her.

Maggie spun around to see Doc Blake grinning at her from under the same Stetson he'd worn that afternoon. She smiled up at him. "Nice hat."

There was an awkward pause when neither of them spoke, almost as if each of them was waiting for the other to make the next move, each staring into the other's eyes. Maggie wondered what it would be like to kiss his lips.

Mr. Kissable broke the spell. "I'm starving for some real food. How about you?"

"You read my mind," she lied. No way did she want him to know what she'd really been thinking.

"Steak?"

"Bloodred."

He chuckled and Maggie wanted to hear more. "There's a table in back with our names on it." He bent his arm out for her to take it. She hesitated for a heartbeat, thinking this might be a mistake, while his smile assured her that she had little choice in the matter. Maggie grabbed hold and walked inside as if she had done it a thousand times before.

When they were seated under the painting of the nude, a smiling twentysomething waitress, dressed in a gray Western shirt, black jeans and the prerequisite boots walked over to take their order.

"Strange to see you here, Doc, on a Sunday night. Dodge burn the roast?"

He tossed her a sly little grin, as if they had a past.

Maggie figured this woman was probably another notch on his already frayed belt. "Not exactly. Let's just say dinner wasn't what I'd expected and leave it at that."

"Gotcha," she said, her face lighting up for what had to be some kind of inside joke.

He turned to Maggie. "What's your poison?"

Maggie smiled and looked up at the red-haired woman, wondering if there were any single women in the entire town who didn't salivate every time Doc Blake was around. "Do you stock any decent wine?"

The waitress ignored her. "Where'd you pick up this one, Doc? Don't think I'm going to like her much."

"Go easy, Helen. She's Kitty's sister."

The waitress turned back to Maggie, looking all apologetic. "Honey, your sister is an absolute treasure. She's been there for me more than once. Because of her friendship, I'm going to give you a pass on your snobby question. How about you give me an order and I go fetch it?"

"A glass of pinot noir." It came out in a whisper.

"I've got a great bottle of Williams Selyem pinot from the Russian River Valley. You'll love it—medium bodied and silky smooth, with a blend of red cherries and raspberries along with a hint of spice. It's dry but the tannins linger on the tongue. It's on the house, honey, as a sort of a 'welcome to the town' kind of thing." She turned to Doc Blake. "That good for you, too?"

"Perfect. Thanks. And two rare steaks with all the trimmings."

"You got it, Doc." She wandered off toward the bar, disappearing into the colorful, raucous mix of patrons.

A cowboy, large both in stature and in girth, stared at Helen, then back at Maggie as he leaned on the bar. Maggie had the feeling he knew Helen well and was protective of her. Mess with Helen and you messed with probably the biggest guy in town.

Maggie threw him a sheepish grin.

He tipped his hat then turned back to his pint.

Maggie wanted to crawl under the table. She was going to have to accept that just because everyone dressed like movie-set ranch hands didn't mean they weren't part of the twenty-first century. She felt completely out of place again, with that familiar knot forming in her stomach.

Doc Blake leaned in closer. "When my patients are as uptight as you seem to be, I tell them to take a deep breath, close their eyes and think of their favorite Disney movie."

Maggie smiled. "Their favorite Disney movie?"

"Yeah, works every time. Trust me on this. Lean back, close your eyes and think of your all-time favorite scene. I know you have one. I can see it brewing on your face."

"What you see is confusion."

"Maybe about which scene is your favorite, but it's there. I know it is."

"From a Disney movie? Not from movies in general?"

"Yup, and don't tell me you weren't a fan of *The Little Mermaid* or *Aladdin*. You're needing a dose of the little girl with the big imagination. I know she's hiding in there, scared to come out. I get a glimpse of her every time you smile. Give it a whirl, Maggie. Just lean on back and close your eyes."

Maggie hesitated, but he persisted, gesturing for her to get going. She figured she might as well go along with him. After all, the man was her new boss. She slid down in the chair then leaned her head back until she found the backrest and instantly felt uneasy, vulnerable, as if everyone in the bar was staring at her.

"This is silly," she said, quickly sliding back up and looking around. Everyone seemed busy with their own lives. No one was the slightest bit interested in what she was doing.

"Silly's the whole idea."

"But—"

"Humor me," he urged, and gestured for her to lean back. She thought she'd better go with it or he might think she was some kind of city snob, which she most definitely was, but she didn't want him to know it. "Take a deep breath. Let your body go all weak and easylike. Breathe in through your nose and let the breath out slowly through your mouth."

Maggie did as she was told. Some country singer was belting out how they loved this bar while Maggie tried to get into the rhythm. Within moments her all-time favorite Disney scene flashed in her head— Beauty and her beast floating across a dance floor. She could visualize them as clearly as if she were watching the movie in a theater. Only difference was, they were dancing to *I Love This Bar*.

She couldn't help but let out a little chuckle.

"I knew you could do it," Doc Blake said as he touched her hand. As soon as he did, she felt warm and safe, as if she had been spinning on the dance floor wrapped in his arms.

She opened her eyes.

Helen had returned and busied herself pouring wine into their glasses. When she left, Maggie said, "I'm sorry, Doctor Granger, I think I fell asleep for a moment."

"Call me Blake. It's easier. Do you feel better?"

"Much. Thanks. Do you work this kind of magic on everyone?"

"Not everyone. Some of my patients are stubborn."

"More stubborn than me?"

"You're easy."

She felt the heat of a blush. "Not necessarily. It depends on the man."

"So we're back to that, are we?"

"Not if you don't want to be."

He grinned, and his whole face lit up, the tiny lines around his eyes adding to his rugged charm.

"In all honesty, I was on my way to talk to you."

As Maggie looked into those smoky eyes of his she had a feeling she could easily fall hard and fast into the same trap all the other women in this town had willingly fallen into. She refused to let it happen. She would not lose her heart to another unattainable man, especially not her boss. She'd been down that road before and it wasn't pretty.

"Talk to me about what?" she asked after she picked up her glass of wine and took a sip.

She reminded herself that she had not come to this bar or this town to fall in love. Not that she was even close to falling in love, but just in case her heart wanted to go there, she needed to confirm it to herself that love or lust or affection of any kind was not part of this potato adventure. Hard work and a paycheck were all she needed at the moment…and maybe another glass of wine and the occasional steak.

But that was it.

Nothing and no one else.

"Mrs. Abernathy," he said.

She drank several big gulps of the deep red elixir before she noticed its full rich flavors of oak and black cherries dancing on her tongue. The mixture of the wine, the devilishly striking man sitting across from her and the unfamiliar ambiance of country music and laughter felt intoxicating.

"What about Mrs. Abernathy?"

Their food arrived and suddenly Maggie remembered how much she loved a good, rare steak.

"She's Tim's great-aunt," he said. "And she's tone deaf."

The meal smelled and looked delicious, but the man sitting across from her was looking even more delicious, especially under that old hat. Who knew a cowboy hat could make a man be so enticing.

"Kitty's mentioned her. That's too bad," Maggie told him, not understanding the relevance.

Blake took note of her plate of food. "You're gonna love this."

"I'm sure I will."

And as simple as that, Maggie knew what all the other women in the town had known all along. Doc Blake was sinfully irresistible.

HE HAD DRIVEN into town precisely to fire Maggie Daniels. Had gone over what he was going to say a dozen times, and if he hadn't stopped at Belly Up for a steak first, he would have been able to carry out his plan to tell Kitty of his decision. He had wanted to avoid meeting up with Maggie altogether.

The whole idea of firing anyone, much less Kitty's sister, gnawed at him terribly. But Kitty already knew about his confrontational misfortune, and would have broken it to her without too much coaxing. Then he would have driven over to Mrs. Abernathy's house—calling her wasn't an option—and given her the good news.

Unfortunately, Maggie had been standing in the doorway of the Belly Up, smelling like a wild rose garden after a rainstorm, and messed up everything.

Sharing a meal with Maggie Daniels somehow felt just about perfect to Blake. One look at her and he knew his hunch had been right. He'd hoped that once she'd lost that corporate suit and heels Maggie would be as down-home as her sister, minus the organic-vegan thing.

Maggie was a good ol' girl at heart, who could probably knock back a cold one with the best of them, if it ever came to that. But right then, sitting across from her, he knew getting her to drink a beer was out of the question. She was still carrying around the city in her back pocket, and as long as she did, Briggs was simply a town where her baby sister lived.

There was nothing he could do about that, and besides, who was he to point out that life in a small town beat city life any day of the week. He'd already been down that path with his ex. He'd met her in college, at UCLA. She'd grown up in L.A. and had told him she wanted a simpler life. He believed her. She lasted in Briggs for only a short time and soon after Scout was born, she wanted to move back to California. Blake obliged, but he never took to the place, and Bethany eventually lost interest in being a mother—at least, not the kind of mother Scout needed. That lesson was enough of a burn in one man's life. He wasn't about to go close to the fire again.

Now, he had to let Maggie go before she'd even set foot in his office. It was for the best, all around. He had to tell her, but telling her face-to-face seemed almost impossible.

He'd have to man up for his daughter's sake. Maggie was danger personified. Scout needed a mother, someone more like Helen and not a woman like Maggie. Helen was stable, kind, and sure as rain she wasn't going anywhere. Helen could love Scout—heck, she probably already did—and could easily be a good mother to his sweet little girl.

Maggie was an unknown—albeit an attractive unknown that sent his pulse racing and weakened his resolve with every heartbeat. But even though she was temptation in borrowed boots, he wouldn't allow himself to put his daughter through another disappointment, so he buttoned up his emotions and moved on with dinner.

He watched Maggie pack it away as if she'd been without food for weeks. "How's the steak?"

She gazed up at him with a look on her face that told him it was the first time she'd noticed he was still there since the plate of food had been placed in front of her.

Maggie paused for a moment, chewed and swallowed. "Amazing. I mean San Francisco has some great steaks, but, *wow*..."

He watched as she took another bite. "So this is your first real meal since you've been here, right?"

Maggie nodded, her mouth once again so full of food she looked like a cartoon chipmunk. She chewed and swallowed while Blake waited, enjoying watching her try to appear like she had everything under control...which she didn't. "How did you know?"

"I know your sister, remember?"

Maggie nodded and swallowed, then took a long draw of wine.

He said, "I love a woman with a hearty appetite. You want me to order another steak in case that's not enough?"

She put her fork down and sat back with a sigh. "Sorry. I love my sister, so don't get me wrong, but if I have to eat one more piece of soy chicken or a beef-like product I might have to disown her."

"What do you think brought me in here tonight?"

"Tell me she didn't—"

"She did. A tofurkey."

"I'm sorry."

"Not a problem. It was better than her flourless cake for my birthday last year."

"Crazy as it seems, I now know how to make one. You don't treat me right and I'll bring one into the office."

Blake emptied his glass of wine and poured another then topped hers off. "Funny you should mention the office. There's something I need to tell you."

"About Mrs. Abernathy?"

"Who? No. This is something entirely different."

"Another rule you and Kitty left out?"

"Not exactly." He hated this kind of stuff.

"If it's about the cake, I promise not to bring one in,

or anything else that's even remotely good for you. But you realize my sister will probably outlive us both."

"I know. She's a regular food doctor."

"Yeah." Maggie sliced off another piece of steak. "But we'll have so much more fun."

That brought on an actual giggle and Blake couldn't help but notice how deep that dimple was in her left cheek, and how downright pretty her eyes were, and how her forehead wrinkled, and how he was thinking about what it might be like to kiss those full lips.

He had it bad and he barely knew the woman.

Blake forced himself to look at the line dancers in front of him. The place was jumping tonight, and for a Sunday that was a rare occasion. Briggs was gearing up for Spud Week and the harvest. Two things that put happy in everyone's heart.

The thought made him smile, and as he watched the couples kickin' it up, he decided that as soon as Maggie gobbled down the last bite, he'd ask her to dance. One dance couldn't hurt.

Then he'd fire her.

And just as he considered how he would accomplish these tasks, her cell phone chirped.

"Excuse me," she told him and took the call. In seconds her entire demeanor changed. "I'll be right there." She stood. Her napkin fell to the floor. She looked at Blake and her eyes went moist.

He felt his stomach tighten. "What's wrong?"

"That was a nurse at Valley Hospital. Kitty's been admitted. I have to go."

"I'll drive you."

And before Blake could think of what this might mean, he and Maggie were in his pickup racing toward the hospital.

Chapter Four

Valley Hospital was bigger than Maggie had expected. She somehow had a preconceived idea that any hospital in this minor town would be small and inadequate. On the contrary, it took up about a half-acre of land, had four floors and a staff that seemed as professional as any hospital the Bay Area had to offer.

Fortunately, Doc Blake was the calm breeze to Maggie's hurricane of emotions and knew exactly where to go and who to ask about Kitty. For the most part, he didn't exactly have to ask anyone anything. Maggie witnessed firsthand the benefits of living in a small town.

"Hey, Doc, Kitty's up on the third floor in maternity," someone behind a desk shouted as he and Maggie walked into the E.R. waiting room. "Room three-twenty-four, but she's just getting up there so it might take a bit before you two can see her."

Blake nodded. Maggie hadn't taken another step, though, when several people wanted to meet Kitty's sister. Maggie was cordial with the introductions while her mind raced through countless scenarios that her sister might be dealing with.

One of the people in the waiting room was an older

woman. She didn't appear to be an E.R. patient, rather, someone who was waiting for a loved one already inside. She walked up to Maggie and wrapped her arms around her, giving her a tight hug. "Don't you worry about nothing, honey. Nothing bad's gonna happen to your sister or them babies. They got the best doctors in all of Idaho working at this here hospital, so you just keep smiling 'cause that's what your baby sister needs right now."

For some inexplicable reason, Maggie believed her and held on tight for a moment before she let go. "Thanks."

"Whew. Take it easy, honey. These bones of mine are getting mighty fragile," the woman said. Then she looked over at Doc. "You gonna make a formal intro or do I gotta do it myself?"

Blake chuckled and said, "Mrs. Abernathy, this is Maggie Daniels. Maggie this is Mrs. Esther Abernathy."

"Don't mumble, son. Speak up."

Maggie raised her voice a couple of decibels. "Doc Blake has mentioned you. It's great to finally meet you."

Esther turned to Blake. "I can hear her perfect. Why can't you learn to talk like that?"

She didn't wait for Blake's response. Instead, she turned back to Maggie. "What your sister is gonna need is complete bed rest till it's safe for them babies to be born. She's been having contractions for the past couple weeks and the poor thing didn't know it. Caused her cervix to flatten to one-point-two centimeters. Not good. They pumped her full of terbutaline to stop them contractions and a corticosteroid to get them babies' lungs to mature...just in case.

"But we're not going to dwell on that possibility now. If everything goes good, and there's no earthly reason why it won't, 'specially if I have anything to do with it, they'll be letting her out of here in a few days. Once they do, I'll be stayin' right there with her to make sure she don't get out of bed but to use the facilities and to bathe once in a while. I'll need my own room, so honey, if you're sleepin' in the guest room, you're gonna have to move on out. Sorry to put you in such a pickle, but I'm the only one who knows how to handle a spitfire like Kitty. Maybe you can sleep on Kitty's sofa, but if I remember right, that sofa's made out of materials that no man or beast can get themselves comfortable on. You might think of gettin' a room somewhere. Or—" she turned to Doc Blake "—she can move in for a spell with you and Dodge. You got that nice big spare bedroom your ma kept that ain't doin' you no good. Your ma would've liked to see a pretty little thing like Maggie using it, instead of that nasty old wife you once had messing it up for some kind of business office that wasn't never no business worth a lick.

"Now you two go on up to Kitty's room and quiet yourselves. She needs her sister to hold her hand for a spell and to tell her everything is gonna be just fine. I got to go home now and start packing and preparing before I can move into that all-natural house. It won't be easy, but when God gives me a challenge I got no choice but to follow through, 'specially since tolerating Kitty's 'green' ways is His way of getting me closer to heaven."

Then, as if that was all that needed to be said, Esther Abernathy abruptly turned and walked off, leaving Maggie and Doc Blake standing in the middle of the room wondering what the heck had just happened.

BLAKE SAT ON A hard chair against the wall in the tiny private room at Valley Hospital trying not to fall asleep. It had been almost five hours since they'd arrived, and the last time he'd checked, Maggie still wasn't comfortable leaving her sister. She'd been sitting next to her sister's bed, holding Kitty's hand for almost four hours straight. Blake didn't have the heart to try and convince her to leave, so there they both sat watching Kitty sleep.

Maggie's reaction and her dedication to Kitty had thrown him for a loop. Up until that urgent phone call, he had expected Maggie to react to these types of emergencies exactly as his ex-wife had, cool and indifferent. Even when Scout broke her arm at daycare, it was Blake who went rushing to the hospital to be with his child, not Beth. She had waited until that night to comfort Scout, when all the urgency was over and Scout was sleepy from the pain medication.

That had been the final blow to their marriage. Blake knew right then and there he couldn't continue to live with a woman who put her own needs before their daughter's. Beth had chosen to remain at work and have Blake handle it, rather than finding out what Scout needed.

He had filed for a divorce the very next day.

The door opened and a dark-haired nurse Blake knew well walked into the room. "You two should go home," she whispered. "Kitty's contractions have slowed way down. Those babies aren't going anywhere tonight. You can come back in the morning when Kitty's awake. She'd probably like that much better. Right now she has no idea you're here. Besides, Doc, my son Conner has an appointment with you tomorrow afternoon and I'm sure he'd like it much better if you weren't sleepy when you have to extract his wisdom teeth."

Blake stood, stretched then settled his hat on his head, walked over to Maggie and held out his hand to her. "She's right. We should go."

Maggie looked up at him, her eyes still red from crying. Makeup completely gone. He wanted to take her in his arms and comfort her, but he knew he couldn't. Not now. Not like this.

"You can leave, but I want to be here when Kitty wakes up." She turned back to her sister, ignoring his outstretched hand.

Blake gave the nurse, a woman he had dated briefly when they were in their early twenties, a pleading look. She walked over to Maggie, and gently patted her back. "Maggie, I'm Cori. Tim's cousin." Maggie stood and they gave each other a tight hug. "Believe me, sweetie, I know how you're feeling." Maggie went back to sitting next to Kitty. "I have a sister, and if she were in here I'd want to camp out as well, but it's really better for everyone if you go home and get some rest. That way, if she needs you in the morning, you'll be clearheaded."

"We always promised each other that if anything ever happened to one of us, we'd be there. I have to stay. I promised."

"But nothing's happened. And nothing's going to

happen. Not on my watch. Kitty's fine. So are her babies."

"How can you be sure? What if those contractions start up again?"

"Trust me. I've been taking care of pregnant women for the last eight years. As long as she stays down and takes her meds, everything will be just fine. I promise."

Blake had to admit the whole thing made him nervous. He'd already been through a birth tragedy with Colt's wife, when Joey was born. But he knew this was different. For one thing, Kitty was in much better shape than Colt's wife had been. And Kitty wasn't hemorrhaging, she had merely started labor six weeks too soon. Plus, he knew Cori wouldn't make a promise if she thought she couldn't keep it. She was a straight shootin' kind of girl. Always had been, and probably always would be. It was her brutal honesty that Blake had had a hard time with when he was dating her. However, over the years he'd come to realize that Cori's honesty was a dependable force.

He once again held out his hand to Maggie. This time she took it and stood, facing Cori. "Are you here all night?"

"Until nine when my shift is over. I promise I'll call your cell or I'll call over at the house if anything changes. But nothing's going to change. Kitty and those babies mean a lot to our family, so let me do my job."

"No matter how small, you'll call me?"

Cori nodded. "You have my word, sweetie."

Maggie bent over and gently kissed a sleeping Kitty on the forehead, then proceeded to head out with Blake by her side, still holding her hand. He threw Cori a smile and a nod as he left.

"Get yourself some sleep, Doc. Conner doesn't need any slip-ups with that extraction."

"I intend to do just that."

Her gaze shifted to his hand still holding Maggie's, and she threw him a wry look. "I'm going to try to believe you."

He let her comment slide. Maggie didn't seem to hear it and he was in no mood to defend his ethics.

They didn't talk much as they left the hospital and drove out of the parking lot, but once they were on the road Blake felt as if he had to break the silent tension. "If you don't want to be alone, you can spend the night with me." She turned toward him, and he caught a look of surprise on her face just as they passed under a streetlight. He thought he needed to clarify. "What I mean is, you can spend the night in the guest room. There's nothing..."

"Thanks, but I just want to go home. I need to email Tim and tell him what's going on. I don't have his address in my phone. It's on Kitty's laptop."

Blake felt dog-tired. It was going on three o'clock Monday morning and he'd been going since five Sunday morning. It had been one of those days that didn't quit, and the thought of driving Maggie home, then driving all the way to the ranch, seemed impossible. The trip would take him almost an hour.

He was thinking of bedding down in the truck, when Maggie made an offer he didn't understand, exactly. "You're welcome to spend the night in my bed."

"I, um, I..."

He glanced over at her and could see the smile slip across her sweet lips. "I'll sleep in Kitty's room. I don't know how far your ranch is, but if you're as tired as

I am, I don't want to be responsible for your falling asleep at the wheel."

How could he resist? "I'd like that. I only have three patients tomorrow, and they start with Conner sometime in the afternoon. I'm not exactly sure what time, but I think we'll be safe if we show up around noon."

"Can I come in a little earlier? I want to get my bearings before any of your patients arrive."

"Whatever makes you comfortable."

And there it was. He decided that Maggie Daniels was nothing like his ex-wife and he wanted her in his office. But, more important, he wanted her in his life.

Still, he had to hold on. He could see himself getting carried away here, only to lose her to the big city. That part of Maggie was ingrained in her DNA. Of that, he was certain. But if a man was worth his name, that man would figure out a way to change her city thinking into Country reason.

Fortunately, he was just the cowboy to do it.

BY THE TIME Blake parked his truck in front of Kitty's reclaimed-brick bungalow, Maggie felt sick with fatigue. She hoped that Blake didn't need much more than to be pointed in the direction of her bedroom and the linen closet, because she was functioning on fumes at the moment.

He followed close behind as Maggie made her way up the brick walkway lined by gold and deep orange baby mums, and up to the cherry-red front door. Kitty's front yard was pretty enough to be in a magazine. Not only was her house *Country Living*–worthy, but her front and backyards could be featured in *Better Homes and Gardens*.

As soon as Maggie opened the front door, flipped on the lights and peeked in the empty living room she felt like crying again. Kitty wasn't there. She was in a hospital fighting to keep her tiny babies inside her.

Maggie couldn't walk inside. Not yet. She turned to face Blake.

"You want, we can sit for a spell on the front porch. Kitty's swing sits two real cozy."

Maggie was tempted. When she'd arrived, she remembered thinking about sitting on that swing, with a cup of steaming coffee, considering what her life had come to. She loved porch swings. When she was a little girl, not long after their father had abandoned them, there was a year when their mom had sent them to live with a cousin in a small town in Indiana. Kitty had taken to it like a kid to Christmas, but Maggie had a tougher time adjusting. Still, the one thing she'd loved about her stay was sitting on that front porch swing, imagining how things would be when she grew up.

Unfortunately, nothing she had imagined had happened, and Kitty's porch swing had turned into a symbol of her failed life, so she wanted no part of it.

They were standing only inches from each other, Maggie totally aware of the concern in his eyes. He took her hand again. She took a step closer, wondering if she should just let go and allow herself to be comforted by this sweet cowboy.

The night felt cool against her skin as the silence that surrounded them seemed to draw them even closer. She wanted nothing more than to fall into his arms and have him assure her that everything was going to be fine. That a lot of pregnant women go through this, it was nothing to worry about. She wanted to kiss

his lips and fall asleep cuddled up next to him, knowing that nothing bad could ever happen as long as she
held on tight.

He took a step toward her.

"That light is keeping me up," Mrs. Abernathy
yelled from somewhere inside the house. "If you're
spending the night, Doc, I made up a cozy spot for you
in the nursery. If not, git goin' with your flirtin' self.
You got patients to deal with later today, and Maggie
don't got no time to be catering to your manly needs
with things like this."

They both laughed. Maggie let go of his hand and
said, "Never could I ever get used to this. How did she
get in here?"

"Kitty probably doesn't lock her doors. Most people
around here don't. It's a courtesy, of sorts. If someone
stops by when you're not home, they can get in and
wait for you."

Maggie shook her head and walked inside. "That's
just crazy. What about killers or crazy people?"

Blake didn't move. "It's a small town. Not too many
of those folks live around here. They usually go for the
anonymity of bigger cities."

Maggie wasn't buying it. At least, not in her tired
state. "Are you coming in?"

"I'm feeling better so I think I'm gonna head on
home. You've got enough going on in this house without me adding to the fuss."

Maggie wanted to tell him to stay. That, if anything,
he seemed to keep her calm. Besides, she had no idea
how to handle Esther Abernathy...*if* she could handle
Esther Abernathy. At the moment, it seemed highly
unlikely. "If you're sure."

He nodded, smiled and tipped his hat. "I'm sure. You have a good night, Maggie. Don't worry about a thing. Kitty couldn't be in better hands. I'll see you later, then."

Blake hesitated for a second, and Maggie thought he had changed his mind and would come in. Instead, he turned and walked off. She didn't move until she heard the engine on his truck rev up and the sound of the tires on the pea gravel of the driveway, and saw the red taillights disappear into the night.

Maggie suddenly felt wide-awake, and knew the one thing she had to do was email Tim. Once in Kitty's room, her eyes immediately welled up, but she pushed the emotions away with a childhood mantra she and Kitty had made up whenever they didn't want to cry.

"Tuna fish, tuna fish, tuna fish, tuna fish, tuna fish," she said out loud, and it worked. The tears subsided and she sat down in front of the white laptop and brought it to life. She quickly found Tim's email address and began writing, assuring him that although Kitty had had a bit of a scare, she was now being cared for by Nurse Cori, and his great-aunt Mrs. Abernathy, two women who seemed more than capable of getting Kitty and the babies through this temporary blip. Then she typed in her personal email address, wondering why she had never thought to correspond with him before, and ran the spell-checker.

"Tuna fish, tuna fish, tuna fish, tuna fish."

As soon as she had corrected her typos, Maggie let out a sigh, and hit *Send*.

Had she been that busy with her career and her affair with her boss that she couldn't take the time to send her own brother-in-law an email?

Apparently so.

Maggie decided she couldn't sleep in Kitty's bed. Way too emotional for her. So she made her way back to the living room while reflecting on the tuna fish mantra.

It was Kitty who had decided that neither one of them could cry when they were thinking about tuna fish. They both hated tuna, especially canned tuna, because for about two years straight it was practically all their mother served them. Money was tight, and Mom had made it her protein of choice, even adding it to mac-and-cheese and pasta sauce.

The thought made Maggie cringe.

Once in the living room, she remembered that Mrs. Abernathy had warned her about sleeping on the green sofa, and she knew that sleeping in the nursery would be even worse than Kitty's bedroom. Instead, Maggie switched off the light, grabbed the quilted throw off the sofa, stepped out onto the front porch and decided it was time to sit on that swing.

She approached it slowly, wondering if this was a smart move. Then, without allowing herself to dwell on the past and what might happen in her future, she merely sat down, tucked Kitty's decorative pillows under her back and head, and wrapped the blanket around her, forming a barrier between herself and the cool night air. The moon gave everything a soft white sheen, and the complete silence seemed almost surreal to her. No car horns, no sirens blaring in the distance, no foot traffic, just an occasional cricket and the gentle flutter of the breeze hitting the tall trees that surrounded the house.

She figured the neighbors across the street and next

door must still be sleeping. Their homes were dark. Everyone in this neighborhood lived on an acre or two of land, so even if they were awake and busy with their mornings, Maggie wouldn't be able to hear them.

When she had first moved in with her sister, a little over a week ago, she didn't like the feeling of being so separated from other people, but as the days slipped by Maggie had begun to appreciate the distance. It gave her a sense of peace, a sense of privacy that she was starting to value.

Maggie sat back and felt the tension drain from her body. Ever since her first night in Idaho, the night sky had dazzled her. She never imagined there were that many stars in the entire universe, let alone in the sky over Briggs. She could now see why Kitty loved it here so much. Sitting out on the swing, in the quiet of the night, Maggie felt connected, a part of the world around her.

As if she belonged.

But as soon as the thought whisked through her mind, another one popped in. How was that feeling even remotely possible? She was a true city girl to her core. She didn't know the first thing about country living, about snakes, and mice or the bigger critters that roamed this part of the world.

And she especially didn't know the first thing about Doctor Blake Granger, a cowboy turned dentist.

She slipped down on the swing, gave herself a tiny push, then propped her head on a cushy pillow and closed her eyes. She had the feeling daylight was about to slip over the mountains at any moment, but she wasn't even remotely ready for its arrival, not to mention what the day had in store for her.

Chapter Five

When Blake finally opened his eyes sometime around ten-thirty in the morning, he felt as if he'd been hit with a John Deere tractor then dragged for twenty feet. It didn't help that Scout had the need to jump on his back while Suzy nuzzled and licked his face.

"Time to wake up, Daddy. Grandpa says the kitchen's going to close in ten minutes, and if you want breakfast you'd better hurry up."

Blake pulled his pillow over his head, causing Suzy to be more determined to get at him. Then Mush jumped up on the bed, barking and tripping over Blake's legs.

"Wake up, Daddy. Wake up."

Blake rolled over and took the blankets with him. Scout slipped off his back. Then he rolled again, and landed on the floor with a thump.

That did it. He was awake now.

He could hear Dodge's voice growling from the stairway, "Stop horsin' 'round and git down here. I got more important things to do than cook for a lazy son who stays out half the night wooin' the new girl."

Blake didn't have to think twice about how Dodge already knew he had been with Maggie last night.

Someone from the hospital probably phoned him at dawn giving him the scoop. Might have even been Cori herself. She and Dodge were buddies.

Mush licked his face in one great big wet swipe. Blake pushed him away as Scout jumped on Blake's belly. It was enough to make a man scream in pain. "I'm up. I'm up." He looked at his smiling daughter as she sat contentedly on his T-shirt–clad chest.

"Then get up, Daddy. Grandpa said he'd give me another flapjack if I brought you downstairs, and I want that flapjack real bad. It has blueberries in it and I love blueberries."

Scout was still clad in her Sheriff Woody pj's, hair in its usual whirl of curls and knots, and a thin smear of berry jam on her left cheek. If he loved his child any more than he already did, he'd burst. "Then we'd better hop to it, baby. You run downstairs and tell your grandpa to stop his bellyaching. I'll be right there."

Scout jumped up with a squeal of delight and headed out the door, the dogs following close behind, while Blake contemplated the roller-coaster of emotions he'd gone through the previous night. First up was his strong desire to keep Maggie right there in Briggs…like that was going to be an easy task. The woman couldn't see what was as clear as a new moon shining down on fresh snow. She had a Country heart, and there was no amount of city that was ever going to change that.

"You better make it soon, son," Dodge yelled up the steps. "Your wooin' gal just pulled up in a fancy car, and looks as if she's loaded for bear."

Maggie had arrived way too early, and what was even worse, he wasn't nearly ready to see her again.

Blake jumped up, went over to the bank of windows in his bedroom that overlooked the front of the house and carefully opened the shutters to take a peek. Sure enough, Maggie Daniels, clad in casual business clothes and cowboy boots, had parked her fancy car and was now walking toward the house.

"Darn it all," Blake mumbled to himself. "That woman has a willful mind."

He hurried into the bathroom to take a quick shower. He couldn't possibly let her see him when he felt so lousy. A shower was a necessity, especially if he wanted to be able to think straight.

He could only hope Dodge, the dogs and Scout didn't scare her away.

MAGGIE TOOK A deep breath and slowly let it out as she climbed the front stairs of Blake's porch. The ranch house was bigger than she had expected, and much more civilized-looking than her imagination had conjured up. Old Westerns hadn't prepared her for this kind of rugged charm.

Sure, the redwood logs needed staining, and the floorboards should be refinished, but the structure of the house, with its solid wood and hard tile roof put it right up there with some of her favorite architecture of all time. Not to mention the location of the house itself.

It had a three-sixty view of the entire valley from the wraparound porch. Plus, she could see the majestic Teton mountain range in the distance. A cool fall breeze rushed around her, bringing on a pleasant shiver. She loved this time of year more than any other and if she wasn't such a city girl, she could totally get how Kitty might have been swept away by the beauty of it all.

The butterflies in her stomach only added to the tension she was already feeling about her first day. Or maybe it wasn't the job that was making her so shaky.

Maybe it was seeing Doc Blake again.

Maggie had given him a lot of thought the previous night, mostly smoldering bedroom thoughts that had made her heart race and kept her from falling asleep until dawn touched the sky.

Mrs. Abernathy had awakened her at seven-thirty that morning with a cup of real, honest-to-goodness coffee and a raisin-bran muffin from Holey Rollers. The coffee was strong and the muffin was delicious, especially warmed and spread with fresh butter. As far as Maggie was concerned, the woman was a saint, and giving up the guest room was the least she could do for her.

An hour after indulging in three cups of coffee, calculating she was going to need it, Maggie and Esther—they were on a first-name basis now—took off for the hospital to visit Kitty.

Much to Maggie's relief, Kitty was sitting up in bed eating a breakfast of poached eggs, raw spinach and quinoa—a tasteless, high-protein grain—courtesy of a vegan neighbor.

An hour after that, Esther chased Maggie out of the room so Kitty could catch up on her sleep.

Maggie didn't want to drive back to Kitty's for fear she'd fall asleep on that swing again and miss her start time at the office. So she drove directly to Doc Blake's ranch and there she stood, on his front porch, an hour early, with butterflies in her stomach and wondering if she was in the right place.

The front door opened and a gruff-looking older

man, with shaggy strawberry-blond hair and a crooked
smile, stood in its frame. She noticed right off that he
had kind eyes and looked an awful lot like an aging
Doc Blake.

"Well, come on in, honey. You ain't gonna get
nothin' but cold out there."

"Thanks, but maybe I'm not in the right place. I'm
Maggie Daniels, Kitty's sister and—"

"Honey, there ain't no doubt in my head that you
and Kitty are kin. It's all over you like clothes on a
line. Now you come on in here. I'm Dodge, Blake's
dad on his good days, and a pain in his butt on bad
days. I was just about to put breakfast on for that son
of mine who can't seem to git hisself outta bed on such
a fine mornin'. But, I'm thinkin' now that you're here,
he'll be high-tailin' it down those stairs any minute
now. How 'bout a nice cup'a coffee? You look like you
could use one."

Maggie didn't hesitate. Coffee could lure her into a
lion's den. "That would be perfect," she told him as she
walked inside. The house smelled of bacon and maple
syrup, two culinary delights she would give her left
arm for…well, maybe not her left arm, but her Coach
purse could easily be swapped.

She followed him through the living room, a rich
blend of dark woods, comfortable-looking chairs and
sofas, red blankets and decorative pillows. A massive
two-story stone fireplace anchored the room, and book-
shelves loaded down with hard-back books covered
three walls. What she didn't see was any taxidermied
wildlife, a relief if ever there was one.

An adorable little boy with a mess of strawberry-
blond curls sat at the table swinging his legs, totally

focused on what he'd just finished eating. His hair caressed his cherub face in a long tangle of curls, and
she noticed he wore Sheriff Woody pj's.

"Scout, where's your manners?" Dodge asked. "This
here's Kitty's sister. You be nice to her and say hello."

"That's okay. I can see he's busy eating," Maggie
said.

Scout chuckled and looked over at Maggie. "I'm not
a boy. I'm a girl. My hair's too long to be a boy. I want
to get it cut, but my daddy won't let me."

Dodge pulled out a chair for Maggie.

"My mistake. Sorry." She winced at her gender
blunder, then sat one chair away from Scout and set
her purse under the chair. "Why would you want to cut
your hair when it's so pretty?"

"It gets in my eyes when I'm playing with my cousins."

Maggie picked up her purse off the floor, opened
it and dug around for her pouch of hair accessories.
"I have just the thing to help with that." Maybe if she
came to the little girl's hair rescue, it might minimize
mistaking her for a boy, which was a pretty embarrassing first meeting. As usual, she never said the right
things around kids.

Scout put her fork down, slid off the chair, walked
over to Maggie and peeked inside her purse. "Wow,
you have a lot of things in there."

Dodge placed a blue mug of steaming coffee and
an empty plate down in front of Maggie. "Black or
the works?"

"The works, thanks," Maggie said. She pulled out
three tiny pink clips, a lavender band and a small dragonfly barrette and laid them on the table. As she placed

everything in a neat row, she asked, "Which do you like best?"

Scout studied the assortment for a long time. Then she said, "Do I have to choose? I like all of them."

She should have known better than to ask a child to choose. "Okay, then we'll use them all." She pulled out a brush, and some tangle spray. Maggie was nothing if not prepared for hair emergencies. "Let's go into the bathroom, so we don't get any hair on the table."

Scout took Maggie's hand and led her to the bathroom. Maggie felt thrilled that this little girl seemed to like her, but apprehensive, as well. Never had any child been so sweet. She warned herself not to get too happy over it. No way could it ever last. Children were impossible to understand, and their behavior never made sense to her.

Still, she liked the way Scout's warm hand felt in hers, almost as if it were a natural kind of event that she could get very used to.

Within a few minutes Maggie had Scout's hair combed and styled with a small braid that draped down the side of her head. Pink clips held the top in place and the dragonfly barrette decorated the bottom of the braid. Then she took a clean hand towel, wet it in the sink and washed the jam off Scout's cheek, along with any other food that was stuck to her sweet face.

When she finished, Maggie turned Scout toward the mirror over the vanity so she could see herself. "What do you think? Too much?"

Scout stepped up on a pink plastic stool to get a better look. She took a deep breath, twisted her head from side to side to assess the do, then said, "Now it won't get in my eyes. My mamma used to fix my hair when we lived in L.A. Daddy says she's too far away to do it now, but when she comes to visit she promised to fix it every day. Could you show her how? I really like all the clips and the barrette. A lot."

She turned back to face Maggie, and without thinking Maggie bent over and they hugged. It was the first real hug Maggie had ever received from a child, and perhaps the best hug she'd ever experienced, especially now when she was so worried about Kitty. It was almost as if Scout knew she needed a bit of loving and hugged Maggie extra-tight.

"WELL, DON'T YOU look like a little princess," Blake said to Scout as she and Maggie walked hand-in-hand back to the table. He couldn't believe the difference in his child with just a bit of hair care. She looked like a delicate little girl, not the scruffy tomboy who usually ran around the house, despite her boyish pj's.

"Maggie fixed my hair. Isn't it beautiful?" Scout twirled to give him the full effect.

"Perfect," Blake told her. "Did you thank her?"

Scout instantly went to Maggie, who was taking her seat at the table. "Thank you, Maggie. Can you come by every morning to fix my hair?"

"Scout, I—" Blake tried to intercede, but Maggie answered before he could finish his sentence.

"If you'd like me to, sure, but I can only do it on the days I come in to work for your dad. Will that be okay?"

"That's perfect, Maggie. My hair will need a rest by then, anyway."

Dodge approached the table carrying a high stack of flapjacks on a plate. "Well, don't that beat all. Scout, you look pretty 'nough to be on a magazine cover in a grocery store."

Scout scooted back up onto her chair. "Maggie did it, and she's going to fix my hair every morning, except on the days she doesn't work in Daddy's office. Isn't she nice, Grandpa?"

"Too nice," Blake said. He watched Maggie add cream to her coffee from the white cow pitcher on the table, along with a couple of teaspoons of raw sugar from the sugar bowl Dodge normally kept hidden in the pantry.

"May I have one more?" Scout asked her grandpa. "You should have one, Maggie. I can't get enough of 'em."

Maggie nodded and forked two onto her plate, then smeared on butter, drenched them in maple syrup, and took a monster bite. One thing was true about this woman, she could eat more food than most men he knew and still fit into those tight jeans of hers. He wondered how that was even possible. His ex hardly ate, and when she did, it was usually only a few bites and she'd claim she was full.

But not Maggie.

"These pancakes are amazing!" she said after she swallowed an enormous bite.

Dodge pulled up a chair and sat down right next to her, while Blake sat at the opposite side of the table.

"'Round here we call 'em flapjacks, and I been makin' 'em ever since my daddy taught me how on a cattle drive in Montana when I was no bigger than a frog in a pond," Dodge said.

He liked to brag about his flapjacks, saying he had a secret ingredient that made them taste better than most. Dodge swore he wouldn't tell anybody what that ingredient was even if a person was on their deathbed, begging. The man took his cooking seriously.

"Well, your *flapjacks* are amazing, and the blueberries are as sweet as honey."

Dodge was hooked. Blake could see it on his face. All anybody had to do was tell Dodge that they liked his cooking and he was their friend for life. Maggie had gone beyond just liking it, she had crossed into metaphor, which in Dodge's mind was the ultimate compliment.

Yep, he was hooked, lined and sunk.

"How's Kitty?" Blake asked, wanting to bring Maggie's attention back to him.

"According to her doctor, she's doing really well and should be able to come home tomorrow. Mrs. Abernathy has everything under control at the house, so I'm not worried. But I'd like to thank you for being there last night. You helped keep me from having a complete meltdown."

"Anytime."

And there it was. That look Maggie had, the one that showed off her down-home goodness, and would have brought him to his knees and had him pleading for a kiss if his daughter and father weren't in the room. He didn't know if it was the dimple, or the way the light caught in her eyes, or the sweetness of her lips, but whatever it was, he wanted to see more of that look on a daily basis.

"Well," Blake said as Maggie shoved the last of her flapjacks into her mouth. "We better get into the office so you can get settled before our first patient arrives."

Maggie nodded, drank the last of her coffee, grabbed her purse and stood.

"Don't you go lettin' him boss you around, sweetheart," Dodge said. "You just remember what I'm sayin', that boy's all hat and no cattle."

"Thanks, Dad, nice to know whose side you're on."

Dodge poured himself a cup of coffee. "It ain't a matter of sides, son. I'm just sayin' what is."

Maggie chuckled and followed Blake through the living room and out a side door. Blake couldn't wait to get her alone.

As soon as Maggie walked into Blake's dental office, she had the distinct feeling something wasn't quite right. She put her purse down on the desk at the check-in counter where he indicated she'd be sitting, and took the room in.

For one thing, the waiting room had far too many kids' toys scattered around the floor, and far too few magazines.

Then she thought perhaps this room doubled as a playroom for Scout and those cousins she'd mentioned.

When Blake flipped on the lights, she became even more aware of a problem. A plastic, coin-operated, miniature pony ride sat in the corner of the room next to a flat-screen TV that was mounted on the wall, far too low for adult viewing.

That's when she realized what Amanda from Holey Rollers had said: *You're going to come a lot closer than that working for Doc Blake, that's for sure.* Now Maggie realized exactly what she had meant.

Kids!

How could she possibly have missed the connection?

She suddenly felt sick to her stomach.

Blake stood at her side, wearing that same look he'd given her the previous night—all sexy cute.

"Maggie, I—"

But Maggie was in no mood for flirting. "Tell me you're not a pediatric dentist, and that this is space for Scout to play in, and not your waiting room."

Blake's demeanor instantly changed and his forehead wrinkled. "She plays in here occasionally, but only when I'm working, and of course I'm a pediatric dentist. That's what I do. I work on kids' teeth."

Maggie frowned at the whole concept. The mere idea she would be working with children freaked her out. Kitty had *not* prepared her for this. She took a step back. "You can't be serious."

"Look around you. Do you really think I cater to adults? An adult wouldn't even fit in one of my dental chairs."

"You lied to me. And what's worse, my own sister lied."

She took another step backward, heading for the door they'd come in from. No way was she spending one hour in this office, let alone two or three months.

"I never lied to you, Maggie. And if I know Kitty, she doesn't know how to tell a tall one, at least not with a straight face. I'm thinking it was an oversight."

"She knows how children react to me, and how I react to children. It wasn't an oversight. It was a deliberate attempt to avoid the truth until it was too late for me to bail. And to think I was so upset for her at what had happened last night, and all along she was purposely lying to me."

Maggie crossed her arms over her chest and kept

retreating toward the door. Blake kept moving closer, almost as if he would grab her if she tried to leave. Maggie was beginning to feel trapped, like the room was too small, as if the air was being sucked from her lungs. A feeling she hadn't experienced since she was a teen.

"I can't imagine Kitty purposely lying to you. Did she ever tell you this was an adult office?"

Maggie thought about it. "No, but she never told me it wasn't."

He took another step forward. "Then technically she never lied, she just omitted the details."

"The important details." Maggie's chest was beginning to tighten. "The details that made a difference."

Truth be told, Maggie hadn't spent much time around children, and the little time she had, something always seemed to go wrong. Her very first attempt at babysitting ended in a near tragedy when the neighbor's four-year-old son almost died from eating a hot dog. Maggie had just turned thirteen and was anxious to make her own money. After weeks of nagging, she'd finally convinced Mrs. Turner she was old enough to watch little Matthew. The night started off great until Matthew insisted she prepare hot dogs for his dinner. Not two bites into the dog and he couldn't breathe. Maggie had absolutely no idea what to do, so she picked him up, turned him upside down and shook him. When that didn't work she made him bend over and she patted his back, hard, and the huge bite of hot dog flew out of his mouth.

It was a total accident the child had lived, and when it was over, he kicked her in the shins for allowing him to eat a hot dog when his mother never did.

She didn't babysit little Matthew, or any other child, ever again. Instead, she always kept her distance from them, for their safety, and ultimately, hers.

"Are you all right?" Blake asked just as Maggie faltered.

For some odd reason her right knee seemed to be made out of jelly, and she had to grab the back of a chair, albeit a miniature bright pink plastic one, for balance. She felt as if the entire world had suddenly shrunk to miniature levels and she and Doc Blake were the giants.

"No, I'm not all right. I'm very not all right. Matter of fact, if I don't get some air I'm going to faint on your toddler sofa and it won't be pretty."

"This way," he said, sliding his arm around her waist and escorting her out the front door. The top quarter of the door was made out of glass and, as they approached she could see something or someone peering in at them from the other side.

"There's something out there," she said, and stopped walking. The room seemed to be spinning, so she leaned into Blake to regain her balance.

"It's not real," Blake said.

"Don't tell me it's something stuffed, 'cause if it is, I can't go out there."

"I promise you, it's not stuffed. Trust me."

She turned and looked at him. Her chest felt as if it were in a vise. "Are you…kidding?" she wheezed.

"Let's get you outside."

Maggie had no choice but to trust him, so she closed her eyes and walked out onto the side porch.

Chapter Six

When Maggie had finally taken several big gulps of cool air the tightness in her chest began to ease, and that feeling of being trapped subsided, especially as she moved away from Blake.

The front door to the office was located on the left side of the ranch house, opposite to the main road, but with the same wraparound porch. The monster that had peered in at her through the glass was an intricately carved wooden black bear cub about two feet tall that appeared to be climbing up the center of the door.

Only in Idaho, she thought.

Just then a new bright red pickup came racing around the corner of the house. The female driver parked the vehicle, then jumped out, a wide smile on her round face. She appeared to be in her mid-twenties, wore a white, unbuttoned smock over a gray swirly dress and midcalf gray cowboy boots. "Morning, everybody," she said as she approached. "What y'all standing out here for? We got our first appointment in fifteen minutes."

"Liza, this is Maggie, Kitty's sister and her replacement for the next few months."

Liza smiled and held out her hand. Maggie took

it and Liza gave her a firm but friendly handshake. "Pleased, but those Nezbeth boys'll be here any minute and they're a handful. You good with kids, Maggie?"

Maggie didn't respond and Liza went on without her. "They're enough to test a saint. Best get your patience on with those boys, not that I wanna scare you off or anything, but it's good to know what you're up against before you move in closer."

She smiled, then stepped past them, opened the bear door and disappeared into the office.

"Liza is my dental assistant," Blake said. "And if you didn't catch the caustic resemblance, she's Mrs. Abernathy's granddaughter."

Maggie wanted to smile but she held it in check. Her racing pulse and her inability to truly breathe were still her immediate concerns, especially after hearing about "the Nezbeth boys."

She wanted to lay into Doc Blake for tricking her into this crazy job, even though he technically hadn't tricked her. There was no denying she had a great need for a massive anger vent just as a black SUV pulled up. Nurse Cori stepped out, along with four boys ranging in size from really short to just below Cori's chin.

Maggie suspected these were the dreaded "Nezbeth boys," Nurse Cori's "Nezbeth boys," and one of them must have the wisdom teeth scheduled for extraction. Doc Blake's first appointment. Maggie inched back and pressed her body up against the wall. She needed all the support she could get.

As her gaze rambled past the boys and Nurse Cori, she wondered just how far away those Teton mountains were, and if she started running full-out, how long it would take her to reach them. A person could hide in those mountains and never be found again.

The thought was somehow comforting.

Blake whispered, "Try to be calm for the boys' sake. The oldest can get as jumpy as popcorn on a hot stove, and his brothers tend to follow his lead. So take a deep breath. Relax."

"I'm leaving," she whispered back.

Doc didn't blink. He showed no emotion. He merely said, "Take all the time you need. Liza can fill in for you for a few hours."

Apparently, he didn't get it. "I'm resigning."

He turned to her, grinning. "You're feeling cold-footed. It happens, but I know you can do this, and once you find your backbone you're gonna do just fine." Then he strolled up to the tallest boy and escorted him into the office while the others charged up the porch stairs, almost knocking Maggie over.

She couldn't believe Doc Blake had basically challenged her and calmly walked away.

Who was this man?

"Hey," Cori yelled. "You boys be good. If I hear you were acting up I won't bring you back here, ever." Nurse Cori looked over at Maggie, who was desperately trying to remain calm. "They love coming here. The doc always gives them plenty of trinkets to take home. They're usually pretty good, but don't let them get away with anything or you won't be able to control them. Kitty pretty much lets them do whatever they want as long as they don't kill each other.

"I'll be sitting in my truck reading a book, parked on the other side of the house, if you need me. I don't react well around my boys when they're getting work done on their teeth. Seems I make them even more unruly than they all ready are, so I usually wait outside. They think I'm running errands. Makes them act better if I'm not around. If they get under your feet, don't be afraid to threaten them with a time-out or a good whacking. Just tell them their mom will get out the strap when they get home. Not that I would ever whack my boys. Don't believe in inflicting pain on kids. The threat seems to work, so I roll with it.

"By the way, Kitty's doing great, and I'll be at the hospital again tonight, so don't you worry about a thing. Mamma and babies are going to be a-okay. I promise. See y'all later."

And with that bit of information, or blackmail, depending on how Maggie chose to look at it, Cori pivoted on her boot heel and headed for her black SUV, which she drove around to the other side of the house, leaving Maggie in a pickle, a word she'd come to appreciate.

Maggie took a deep breath, then walked back to the door, and she and the wooden bear peeked inside the waiting room through the glassed-in door. Scout was there, kneeling in front of a bright green table with the smallest boy. The other two boys were busy digging through what looked like saddlebags. Not that Maggie knew the first thing about saddlebags, but she'd seen enough Westerns to recognize them.

Scout suddenly turned toward the door, grinned and motioned for Maggie to come on inside. Her first instinct was still to run screaming toward the Tetons, but that was clearly unrealistic. Then she thought she could simply get in her car and drive away, but she really couldn't do that either. After all, her sister was counting on her to run the office, and Kitty certainly didn't need the added stress of Maggie flaking out on her.

Then there was Nurse Cori, who expected her to handle her boys for the next hour or so. How could she possibly blow that off?

But the biggest hitch was pain-in-the-butt Doc Blake with his "once you find your backbone." Like she didn't have one.

Okay, perhaps he had a point. There was a slight possibility that she'd been lacking a backbone for quite some time. She used to have one. A solid backbone made of steel. Nothing fazed her, she was fearless. Well, maybe not fearless in the strict meaning of the word. More like brave in the face of minor fires, but still.

Scout continued to motion for her to come on inside. Maggie knew she had little choice in the matter without looking like a complete coward, and Maggie Daniels was not spineless. Cautious, perhaps—but definitely not spineless.

Besides, her purse was still sitting up on the counter. She couldn't leave without her purse.

She decided that if one kid threw something at her, screamed for his mother, kicked her in the shins—or worse, bit her—she'd grab her purse and walk. Physical aggression certainly qualified as justification to quit, right?

She'd just have to find her backbone in San Francisco where she belonged.

Maggie yanked hard on the wooden bear, the door swung open, and the kids looked over at her.

She took another deep breath, straightened up and moved forward. Doc Blake would not have the last word on this one.

BLAKE HADN'T HAD time to think much about what Maggie would do concerning the job once he was in his office. He was all work from the moment he slipped on his cowboy-style fringed jacket until his last patient was seen to. Today, that patient was little Tanner Wilson, who needed fillings in both back molars so he could keep those teeth until his permanent molars came in. Tanner was his most stubborn patient, much worse than Cori's kids. Blake liked to book him at the end of the day precisely because Tanner required the most coaxing to sit in the chair, even after his mother had given him the mild sedative Blake prescribed.

Plus, Tanner was by nature a loud, disruptive child who prompted other, calmer children, to act out—especially Scout, who usually ended up crying because Tanner had bullied her. Even Tanner's parents were sometimes helpless when it came to controlling him. Like the song said, Tanner was "bad to the bone," or at least he seemed like it whenever Blake came in contact with him.

Blake stood and stretched, said a quick prayer and went to the waiting room to corral Tanner himself. His assistant, Liza, usually didn't enter the room until Tanner was sedated and lying prone in the chair. She'd already had one too many run-ins with the boy.

When he got to the waiting room, he stopped on a vision he never would have expected. If he'd been a betting man, he would have wagered the ranch that Maggie Daniels would be hiding under the desk by now, with Tanner hanging from the light fixtures.

Instead, Maggie sat cross-legged in the middle of the floor, with Scout sitting on her lap and Tanner sitting next to them, his head leaning on Maggie's shoulder. They looked as cozy as three frogs under a cabbage leaf.

Tanner's nervous-Nelly parents were nowhere to be seen, which probably added to Tanner's peaceful state.

Blake could barely make out the mechanical storytelling voice coming from Maggie's iPad. All three of them were staring intently at the small screen, with the kids taking turns swiping a finger across the device to turn the page.

"What the heck?" Liza said in a low voice as she came up alongside him and saw the miracle in the waiting room. "How is that even possible?"

"Beats me, but I think I need to get to know that woman much better. She keeps surprising me."

Liza stared at Blake. "I do believe you're blushing, Doctor Granger."

"Men don't blush."

"Where'd you hear that?"

"Dodge."

"Ever see Dodge when he's around my gram? He's a regular beet. You got the same skin tone. Must be love, or something like it. Either way, you boys need to strike while the fire's hot or you're both gonna be left out on the range with no cattle."

"Liza, you always did have a way with words."

"It's a gift," she said. "Now get that child in here while he's stupefied so we can fill those molars of his. I got me a date tonight that requires a lot of primpin'.

A girl's gotta look good on a first date or there won't be a second. Not the way the numbers run in this town. We got a genuine lack of good-lookin' eligible men. And most of them aren't wantin' to get married anytime soon. So I've got to get my hot-mamma on or this boy's gonna join the bachelor club for sure."

"Who's the lucky buck?"

She gave him a look. "I don't share that kind of personal information with my employer. At least, not yet."

And she walked off.

Liza just proved that he knew little about how a woman's mind worked. Women, in general, surprised him, especially Maggie Daniels, who one minute was ready to toss her cookies at the idea of wrangling kids, and the next seemed to be the perfect Mary Poppins.

Blake knew when it came to women he was about as in tune as a tone-deaf preacher.

But he had no time to think about that at the moment. Liza was right. He had to get Tanner in the chair before his medication wore off, if he was on medication. There'd been two failed attempts thus far. But Blake was hopeful this time. He'd never seen Tanner so calm unless he'd been drugged.

Blake walked up to the threesome and quickly squatted next to Tanner. "Hey, buckaroo, let's you and me have a talk in my office."

Tanner didn't look at him. "Not now. Maybe when this story's over."

Maggie threw Blake a helpless expression then said to Tanner, "Tanner, Doc Blake's on a schedule and he has to stick to that schedule or his other patients will get mad."

Tanner glanced around the empty room. "There are

no other patients. I'm the last one. I'm always the last one."

"That's true, buddy," Blake said, "so let's get this thing over with, okay? I need to do a little something to your teeth then we can all go home. You can finish the story when we're through."

Tanner shrugged. "I don't want to. I want to finish it now."

"But it's a long story, Tanner, and we just started," Maggie said. "Let's do what the doctor wants. Okay?"

And she hit the power button on her iPad and the screen went black.

Not a good move.

Blake held his breath.

Liza gasped.

Scout murmured, "Uh-oh."

Maggie looked at Blake.

The room was still quiet, and he hoped this might go down easy.

Then it happened.

Tanner screamed as if someone were torturing him, threw himself down onto his stomach, arms and legs waving and pounding the floor. "I won't. I won't. I won't. I want my story. I want my story. I hate everybody."

The door flew open and his mother came running in, yelling, "What are you doing to my son? My poor baby." And she knelt down next to him and began coddling the boy.

Blake fell backward, landing on his butt.

Liza disappeared into one of the patient rooms. Scout jumped off Maggie's lap and moved away from the madness. Maggie stood, seeking the safety of her reception desk.

"I won't! I won't! I want the story! The story!" No matter what his mother tried, Tanner was not about to give up his quest.

Blake scooted away and went to stand next to Maggie, who watched from behind her desk. "This is my fault, isn't it?"

"Not entirely. Likely, his mother once again wasn't able to give him the sedative I prescribed."

Tanner continued to scream. His mother continued to coddle him to no avail.

"Has she ever?"

"Once, but she didn't like the effects."

"What? That he was calm?"

"She likes a spirited child."

A large rubber duck came sailing past Maggie's head and landed on the copier with a loud thunk.

"This can't go on. Do something," Maggie demanded.

"Nothing to do but for everyone to try it again another time."

"And in the meantime, that boy's teeth are rotting and he's getting away with being a bully. I thought you were good with kids."

"I usually am, but Tanner is beyond me."

"And *you* made fun of *my* backbone. Huh!"

To Blake's surprise, Maggie strode toward the waiting room, ducked a flying Mr. Potato Head, and announced, "Tanner, if you don't stop screaming this minute, you won't ever get to know what happened to the knight in King Arthur's Court. I'm going to count to three, and I better hear silence or I'm packing up my iPad and going home. One…two…"

And just like that, Tanner stopped wailing, sniffled, and wiped his hands over his eyes to knock away the tears. He sat up and looked at Maggie.

"…three."

Tanner took in a few ragged breaths.

"My poor baby," his mother cooed.

"Tanner's a knight in training," Scout said. "Not a baby."

"Scout," Blake said, trying to stifle his outspoken daughter.

"She's right," Maggie said. "And as such, he's strong and tough, and can withstand anything, even whatever happens in a dentist chair, right, Sir Tanner?"

No one moved for a few seconds. Tanner sniffled, took a deep breath and let it out. Then he slowly raised himself up, looked at Maggie, wiped his eyes one more time, and proclaimed, "I am Sir Tanner of King Arthur's Court, and the strongest knight of them all!"

He charged across the waiting room, ran around the corner to the open room where everyone could still see him and jumped up into the saddle-brown dental chair as though ready to take on whatever came his way. Liza slipped into the room after him and Scout gave Maggie a thumbs-up, while Tanner's mother sat cross-legged on the floor, looking completely stunned.

Maggie turned to Blake. "So, who has the backbone now?"

He grinned, put his arm around her waist, picked her up and twirled her around. When he finally put her down, he said, "Definitely Tanner, and you, my sweet lady, have true grit."

Then he kissed her. A short little kiss of gratitude, but when he pulled away, he could see she was ready for more, much more.

He wanted to kiss her again, but this wasn't the time or the place. He promised himself he would find both very soon, too, but right now there was a brave knight waiting for his attention.

FOR THE REMAINDER of the week, Maggie familiarized herself with the phone system, the appointment calendar and insurance practices. Kitty was a big help when it came to learning everything. She might have been on strict bed rest, but her phone still worked, and Maggie kept her plugged into her ear at least four hours out of her eight-hour day.

The following week, Maggie became more efficient at interacting with the patients, thanks in part to Scout and her insightful suggestions. Also, Maggie took the time to learn some of the dental procedures that Doc Blake performed on a routine basis, and was pleased to learn that he only used laser technology on the kids to do a filling, therefore she didn't have to endure the sound of drills driving her up the wall.

It was all coming together, except for one little thing: that kiss.

Blake hadn't mentioned it, nor had he tried to kiss her again. It seemed completely odd considering how he'd looked when they had pulled apart. As if he'd *wanted* to kiss her again.

A wave of emotions had swept through her once their lips had touched and she wasn't quite sure how to handle it, but as soon as her feelings had crested, the kiss was over. And now it seemed as though the kiss had never happened.

Was the kiss some sort of local custom she wasn't aware of? Because if it was, she wanted no part of it. Way too much of an adrenaline rush with no payoff.

Not that she was even sure she wanted anything more to come from that kiss, but still…

"If I don't have any more patients, let's close up at noon today," Blake said. Maggie was seated behind her desk, reviewing insurance information. It was Thursday morning and Maggie was wading through all the insurance claims before the weekend. She didn't want to leave anything hanging.

He was acting all professional, at least as professional as any doctor could, all cowboy'd up in a fringed jacket, jeans, black shirt and his favorite scuffed boots. "I've got one heck of a lot to do tonight, and I'd like to get started doing it."

Maggie rolled her chair back and stood. "Strangely enough, you don't have any patients until Monday morning."

"Spud Week. The fair opens tonight. Even the schools are closed. Love to have you on my team tomorrow for the Spud Tug. You win a shiny Spudphy if we win."

Maggie had no idea what the man was talking about. "Let's start at the beginning. What's Spud Week?"

Doc grinned. "If you're gonna spend any time in Idaho, you'll need to familiarize yourself with the almighty spud. Come on over to the fairgrounds later this afternoon and I'll give you a quick course."

"The fairgrounds?"

"Just follow the line of traffic. You can't miss it."

"Not tonight. Kitty's been home for an entire week now, and I have yet to spend any time with her. There's been a nonstop line of friends and family at the front door ever since she left the hospital. We promised each other tonight it'd just be us."

"Sure, but what about Esther? She can be mighty intrusive when she's responsible for someone."

"We've come to an understanding of sorts. Besides, anyone who can transform her entire life to make sure my sister's needs are met is next to sainthood in my book."

"If it gets too much for you we've got a spare bedroom here."

No matter what, Maggie wanted no part of living under the same roof as Doc Blake, even if she had to sleep outside on the swing at Kitty's. It was bad enough that she had to work with him every day, post-kiss. Living in the same house would clearly be a threat to her self-control.

"I put a futon down on the floor in the nursery. I'm pretty comfortable, at least until the babies arrive, but thanks."

Doc stared at her for a second, as if he was about to say something, but then he hesitated. His eyes sparkled and a slight grin warmed his lips…his soft, extremely kissable lips.

"Well, the offer stands," he said, gazing into her eyes as if he truly wanted her to take him up on it.

She knew she couldn't.

Still, the offer was tempting, enough so that if he said one more word…

He abruptly turned and headed for the door, leaving Maggie wondering if there had been a hidden agenda, or if the offer of a room was simply a country courtesy. Either way, Maggie had to catch herself. She had almost given in despite the fact that she had promised herself not to be lured into becoming another of his many lovers, and she certainly didn't need another affair with her boss, especially not this cowboy.

Doc Blake was strictly off-limits.

Chapter Seven

On the drive home, while Maggie should have been thinking about her sister, all she could focus on was remembering Doc's kiss, so sweet and gentle. There had been a fire that sparked through her, wanting him to linger much longer. Plus, she couldn't stop thinking about what it might be like to live at his house for a few weeks, only until Kitty's babies were born. Not just because of Doc Blake, but because the ranch itself was growing on her.

When Kitty had first suggested she come to live with her in Idaho, Maggie had mocked the idea, thinking it was absurd: urbanite Maggie Daniels, living on the open range, under the big sky, with cows, sheep, an abundance of potatoes…and cowboys.

Never going to happen.

But Idaho now seemed like the most beautiful place on earth: the invigorating air, the majestic mountains, the miles of green hills and the Snake River meandering through the valley. In contrast, San Francisco and San Jose, although lovely in their own ways, were tight, crowded and closed in, making it impossible to breathe.

She lowered the windows, took a deep breath and marveled at how delightful her surroundings were. Almost as if she were seeing this part of Idaho for the very first time.

Or was all of this rapture a direct result of that kiss? A kiss that hadn't lasted more than a few seconds. She wondered what she would be like if they ever made love?

She'd probably spontaneously combust.

It was time that Maggie Daniels took the bull by the horns, a phrase she now understood, and stopped pussyfooting around him.

There could be no relationship between them.

Not now.

"Not ever," she said out loud as she pulled into the driveway at Kitty's house and pushed all those thoughts right out of her head. She needed to focus on her very pregnant sister, not on her silly, lusty desire for the country dentist.

She parked in front of the garage, turned off the engine, hopped out and headed for the front door where Mrs. Abernathy was already waiting.

"What took you so long?" she asked as Maggie approached. "You gotta get yourself right over to the fairgrounds with this here potato salad that Kitty made special for the contest. She's determined to take first prize this year, and she can't do that if she don't get this salad entered in the next hour."

Mrs. Abernathy shoved a large red ceramic covered bowl into Maggie's arms.

"What are you talking about? Kitty's cooking? I thought she couldn't stand up long enough to go to the bathroom, much less make a salad? And what contest? Where?"

"Didn't Doc Blake tell you?"

"Tell me what?"

"It's Spud Week, darlin'. The first week of the potato harvest."

"Yes, I know, but—"

"But nothin'. It's the biggest week of the entire year. I'm surprised his office is even open. Usually, the whole town pretty much shuts down for Spud Week. Now you be gettin' along with this here salad. Take it over to booth number six at the grounds. And don't let Phyllis Gabauer cut you off at the pass and start nosin' around askin' what's inside this here bowl. Not that you know, which is probably a good thing. That nosy old biddy. She wins every year by tricking people into telling her what's in their salad. Well not this year. She's in for a big surprise 'cause this is going to be the best salad those finicky judges ever tasted, and Kitty's gonna take home that blue ribbon. Her hubby's gonna be so proud of his little country girl. Now get along."

And she slammed the door shut. Maggie hesitated, then knocked, and Mrs. Abernathy opened the door a crack.

"How's my sister?"

"She's sleeping. You can't see her now, anyway. By the time you get back, she'll be wide-awake and full'a vinegar. You two can catch up then."

She shut the door again, and this time Maggie had no choice but to take the potato salad to booth number six at the fairgrounds, wherever the heck that was.

SURPRISINGLY, JUST AS Doc Blake had said, there was a line of traffic down Main Street. Where they had all come from, Maggie couldn't imagine. She joined the herd, and in less than twenty minutes pulled her car into a slot in a dirt parking lot, grabbed the hopefully soon to be blue-ribbon salad and her purse, then followed the happy group to what appeared to be a small carnival off in the distance.

A fair happened to be the one event Maggie always thought of fondly, more than any night on the town, any concert or cruise. A fair, complete with amusement rides, fortune teller and quilt contest, truly excited the little girl in her. But just like porch swings and lemonade, she thought she had successfully buried those triggers deep in her memory.

The mere idea of a genuine country fair brought up emotions she tried never to dwell on. Good ones, of holding her aunt's hand while they rode the Ferris wheel or played a ring toss game, hoping to win the doll with the pink hair. She and Kitty spending lazy summer days in Indiana, with nothing to do but laugh and play.

She never did win that pink-haired doll. Their mom had come to retrieve her and Kitty before the fair's closing night. Maggie had begged her mom to let them stay one more day, but she wouldn't hear of it. Country life wouldn't do for her girls. They were going to be successful businesswomen with high-paying careers and designer clothes, and a girl could only get those things in a big city.

But at what cost?

She shook away the memories and concentrated on the task at hand: getting Kitty's potato salad to the correct booth.

As she approached the main hub of the fairgrounds, the old familiar scent of fried foods and cotton candy filled the air, causing her to smile with delight.

As country music poured from strategically placed loud speakers, Maggie picked up her pace, thankful she'd worn Kitty's black boots today. Heels would have been a total disaster.

Excitement bubbled up from her tummy, and she felt like a little girl anticipating a magic experience. She wanted to be surrounded by the sights and sounds of a good time.

"What ya got there, honey?" an older woman asked as she walked up beside Maggie, all smiles and warmth.

"A prize-winning potato salad."

The woman arched an eyebrow. "You don't say. So, whatcha' gonna do with that there prize winner?"

"Drop it off at booth six for the contest." Maggie had a funny feeling about this woman.

"What kind'a potato salad is it?"

Fortunately, Maggie had no idea what the salad even looked like. "The winning kind."

The woman smiled. "Mine is, too." And she nodded toward the large black canvas bag she was rolling behind her. "Potato salad can be tricky, especially when you add the mustard. Too much and you lose the sweet flavor of the potato. What kind'a mustard did you use?"

Maggie stopped abruptly to address the woman as they stood at the entrance to the fair. "You must be Phyllis Gabauer. I'm Maggie Daniels, Kitty's sister. Kitty made the salad. I don't cook, unless you want to call toasting a piece of bread cooking. I have no idea what she put in this salad, but according to Mrs. Abernathy, it's good enough to give you a real run for that blue ribbon."

Phyllis straightened up. The friendly smile was gone. "I win this contest every year, honey. There ain't a potato salad in this whole state's better'n mine. I don't care what that bitter nag says." She made a *humph* sound and stalked off. Maggie chuckled.

WHEN MAGGIE DANIELS arrived at the booth carrying a red bowl, Blake figured he'd just struck gold. "I didn't know you knew the first thing about cooking."

"I don't," she said. "This is Kitty's entry."

Maggie handed him the bowl. He took it, but he had his doubts the bowl contained anything even remotely resembling potato salad.

"This can't be good," he whispered.

After dealing with Phyllis, Maggie felt as if she had to defend her sister. "It's going to win the blue ribbon. There is a blue ribbon, isn't there?"

"Yes, but the judges are pretty finicky."

"So I've been told, but this salad is going to please even the finickiest."

"That would be Dodge, and he's a traditionalist when it comes to potato salad. No tofu allowed."

"This is a time-tested recipe, handed down by a woman who has potato salad in her blood." She cocked an eyebrow as if she was hoping he'd believe her.

Blake grinned and handed Maggie a short form. "Fill this out so I can attach it to the bowl. The big tasting is tonight at seven. The winner's announced tomorrow morning, right before the Spud Tug."

Maggie laughed. "A Spud Tug?"

"It's like a tug of war. And the winning team gets a Spudphy."

"I can't even imagine what that might be." She threw him a sly look. He was thinking how he'd love to see this city girl knee-deep in potatoes. Might be kind of cute.

"You'll love it. You can keep it on your kitchen counter to crack open nuts, or knock out an intruder. Hell, I don't rightly know all you can do with the thing, but you'll have fun telling the story of how you won it to all your city friends. Besides, I take my team out to Sammy's Smoke House afterward. Best dang barbeque in all of Idaho. We're needing one more person. What do ya' say?"

She considered it for a full minute, which didn't surprise him. Maggie was like that. She never jumped. Always took her time. He liked that about her, and wondered if that attribute somehow transferred into the bedroom. His ex liked to just get it over with, get the deed done, so to speak. Blake liked to take it slow. Make their time together last, which only aggravated his wife, until they hardly made love at all in that last year. He had a feeling Maggie was the same as he was, slow and easy, like a harvest moon passing over the endless sky.

"Sounds delightful, but I'm not into mud."

"No mud involved."

"Or water."

"No water involved."

"What else—"

He grinned and pushed his hat higher on his forehead. She was nothing, if not ornery.

"Potatoes?"

He nodded. "Mashed."

She paused for a moment, grinned and he knew he had her. "Then you'll be here?" he asked.

"On one condition."

"What's that?"

"We win. I want that Spudphy."

"We'll do our darnedest. The tug starts at two, but you need to be here an hour early to sign in. Plus, Scout's in the Tater Trot and I know she'd love to see you on the sidelines cheering her on."

"I won't even ask what a Tater Trot might be, but anything that Scout is doing I'll most definitely be there to watch."

"Great. See you tomorrow then."

"Tomorrow."

She winked at him, turned and walked away, leaving Blake as happy as a naughty pup with a new shoe.

"WHAT DOES SOMEONE wear to a Spud Tug?" Maggie asked Kitty as they both sat on her bed finishing up the scrumptious dinner that Mrs. Abernathy had prepared for them: baked brook trout smothered in lemon and slivered almonds, fresh green beans tossed with some sort of yummy pesto sauce and berry cobbler topped with rich homemade vanilla ice cream. The woman could not only nurse Kitty but she could cook like a New York chef.

"I can't believe Doc talked you into this. It's almost a miracle of sorts. My sister, Maggie Daniels, willing to get her hair, makeup and designer clothes covered in mashed potatoes. Will wonders never cease?"

Maggie cleared their trays from the bed. "Doc thinks we can win. We're bringing that other team down, baby."

Kitty drank the last of her organic whole milk, wiped her mouth on the checkered cloth napkin she'd made herself and said, "Well, in that case, I'd wear skinny jeans, a pair of my high boots and a T-shirt. I have one from last year's festival that you can have, in case you don't own an actual T-shirt."

Maggie rolled her eyes. "Of course I own a T-shirt." But in all honesty, it wasn't the kind of T-shirt Kitty was talking about. Maggie's little pink shirt cost a hundred and twenty-five dollars, courtesy of Kate Spade, and she wasn't about to get mashed potatoes ground into the fabric...not that it would ever happen, but still. "If you insist. Besides, I won't stand out as much as a tourist if I'm wearing something local."

"It's a small town, sis. You'd stand out even if you wore a potato sack. Which reminds me, I won't get to see the potato sack booth this year and I love all the clever things the Phillips sisters make. Last year I bought a cute little purse and a tea cozy. Maybe you can check out the booth and tell me what they have?"

Not in her wildest dreams could Maggie think of anything that could possibly be labeled "cute" made out of a potato sack. "Not a problem. I'll check it out and report back."

Kitty smiled. "I know what you're thinking, but potato sacks are biodegradable, and besides, I like to support local artists."

"No comment." Maggie held back a giggle.

"Go ahead and scoff, but you'll change your tune once you see everything they make."

"I can't wait."

"Cynic."

Maggie didn't want to argue with her sister. Not tonight. Especially not over potato sack creations. What she really wanted to tell her was how she might be falling for Doc Blake. Not that she would put it that way, exactly. Just that she was definitely thinking a lot about him these days.

Still, she couldn't admit her feelings. That would make them real and she didn't need to pile anything else onto her sister's shoulders.

"You're right. I'm being close-minded…again. I'll check it out."

"Great. You'll see that I'm right. Oh, and you might want to bring a change of clothes. Those mashers can get pretty sticky and smelly once they're on your clothes."

Maggie hopped back on the bed, next to her sister. "That would mean we'd have lost. Never going to happen. Doc promised me a Spudphy, and I intend to hold him to his promise."

Kitty smiled and Maggie's heart soared. She was so happy to see her little sister more like her old self.

"The coveted Spudphy. Now that's something to get excited about. I have just one question."

"What's that?"

"You're not falling for Doc are you? Every time you mention his name your face lights up."

Maggie couldn't look at Kitty, so instead, she fell back on the soft bed. "Don't be ridiculous. He's the town catch and I'm just passing through."

"My point, exactly."

"COME ON, SCOUT!" Maggie yelled as she stood next to Doc while Scout and several other kids her age ran along a short grass track. They were all balancing a big fat russet potato on a large wooden spoon held out in front of them. So far, most of the other kids had lost their potatoes and were out of the race, but Scout and three other little boys seemed determined to make it to the finish line.

Without even thinking about it, Maggie stuck two fingers in her mouth, curled up her tongue and let out an ear-shattering whistle. The high-pitched blast must have hit a chord with Scout because her little feet moved faster.

"I never could do that," Doc Blake said.

Maggie shrugged. "Easy." Then she turned her attention back to Scout, who moved with speed and grace, totally concentrating on the mission with her tiny lips scrunched together, tongue poking out every two seconds, forehead wrinkled, eyes narrowed against the sun and tiny pink cowgirl boots moving in a steady rhythm.

The nearest boy, whose parents wore huge potato-shaped brown hats with smiling faces emblazoned on the front, cheered their son on, their overly loud voices drowning everyone else out.

Maggie had no choice but to whistle again, and once again Scout picked up speed.

"Somehow, I never thought of you as a whistler," Doc told her.

"Tomboy when I was a kid."

"You're the hardest girl to figure out."

"That's my charm."

Scout was only steps away from the finish line, but it looked as if the potato-hat family had their boy pumped up to win.

Then, from out of nowhere, a deep male voice boomed across the field. "You can do it, Scout! Run, girl! Run!" And Scout took off like greased lightning right over the finish line.

The crowd burst into cheers. Even the potato-hat family joined in applauding Scout's achievement.

Maggie let loose a high-pitched whoop, while Doc yelled out his joy over Scout's win.

"Was that Dodge hollering for Scout?" Maggie asked Doc, as they headed for his daughter, now surrounded by well-wishers.

Doc nodded. "He has a way with kids."

"I'll say. Seems like he'd be perfect to help with some of your patients."

"He's been in a time or two."

"Would he consider giving me lessons?"

"Only if you intend to hang around a spell."

"Define *a spell.*"

He turned toward her, sincerity splashed on his face. "A spell in these parts could mean anywhere from a few months to the rest of your life."

She had a sudden urge to wrap her arms around him and tell him the rest of her life would really suit her.

But she said, "That's a fairly broad definition."

He nodded. "Might be, but the way I see it, after a few weeks a person either can't wait to wipe the dust from this ol' town off their boots or they've taken to the place so strong the dust's turned into cracked mud."

Maggie gazed down at Doc's boots. Sure enough, they were the same boots he'd worn every day: scuffed, scratched and now caked with dried mud. Maggie had spent the entire morning polishing Kitty's borrowed boots so even now, as they walked toward Scout on the dirt trail, her boots were as pristine as they had been that morning.

She wondered if Doc had noticed.

As soon as Doc reached Scout, he scooped her up

in his arms and spun her around. "Daddy, did you see me? I won, Daddy. I won!" She held up her Spudphy, her face beaming.

"I saw every minute, baby. You were quicker than a bee buzzing for the hive."

She giggled, and faced Maggie. "I won, Maggie! I won!"

Doc put his daughter down, and she reached out for Maggie. Maggie squatted to her level and gave Scout a tight hug. At once, Maggie felt pure joy as Scout's tiny arms wrapped around her shoulders.

"You were amazing, Scout," Maggie told her.

Scout pulled away and handed Maggie the Spudphy, a four-inch-high silver russet potato with a smiling face, a cowboy hat, and spindly arms and legs. It wore cowboy boots and a belt with an oval-shaped buckle that read BAKER in black letters. Maggie figured the word *baker* on little potato man's buckle was there to remind everyone that a russet was meant for baking, a fact that she had only recently learned. "Isn't it beautiful, Maggie? I never won one of my very own before. Don't you want one, Maggie? It's so beautiful."

"Your dad, here, promised me one for the Spud Tug."

"But you have to win it, and the Spud Tug is hard."

"That'll make it all the better," Maggie said, staring at Blake, who now seemed a bit unsure of himself.

"Not a problem, Scout. Spudphies all around."

But Maggie wasn't so sure.

Chapter Eight

Edith Abernathy sat on a white plastic folding chair in the front row with Maggie Daniels perched right next to her, as a group of stoic-looking judges announced the winners of the various cooking and baking contests. Phyllis Gabaur, who had already won the pie contest, pickle contest and scalloped potato contest, sat at the other end of the row, proudly displaying her blue ribbons that had been pinned across her scrawny chest.

With each announcement, a cheer would rise up from friends and family of the winner. The rest of the anxious audience would offer up their tepid applause, obviously anxious for news of their own entries.

A festive red, white and blue striped canopy shielded the fifty or so onlookers from the hot sun that bore down on the festival like a flashlight from God's right hand. Still, everyone seemed to be in good spirits despite the late-September heat. Blake happened to be one of them. There to help hand out awards, he had tried his best not to give Maggie or Edith a facial hint of who had won the blue ribbon for best potato salad. Truth be told, he didn't actually know who'd won, but he had a strong inkling it wasn't Kitty. He didn't have the heart to tell Maggie, who had seemed so positive that her sister would win.

Not likely.

But he refused to let this one event ruin his enthusiasm or anyone else's, especially since it had been a good day at the fair for the Grangers so far. Scout had won the Tater Trot, and each of his nephews had done well in other events: Gavin had won the potato sack race, little Joey had come in second in the mashed-potato-eating contest, and Buddy, Colt's oldest, had placed in the top two in Spud Idol for his age group. That boy could sing like a young Garth Brooks. Best of all, Maggie had spent most of the day by his side. But now it was time to announce the potato salad winner. He was sure Maggie's attention was about to wane.

The three judges stood at the podium: Dodge, Lindsey Lutz and Jake Barnett, owner of Jake's Old Time Taters and Burgers. If anyone knew potato salad, these three sure did, especially Lindsey, who offered up four different kinds for every church event Our Lady of the Tetons had to offer.

Dodge stepped forward and spoke into the microphone. In front of him, a table held an assortment of yellow, orange and blue ribbons.

"Testing," he said in his low, booming voice.

The audience answered with a resounding, "We can hear you!"

Blake felt his stomach lurch. He couldn't believe this contest was having such an effect on him. Maggie looked over at him with those big blue eyes and that delicious mouth. He tried with everything that was strong in him not to react, but his emotions betrayed him and a darn smile spread across his lips.

"Let's get on with it, then. First I want to say that this year's crop of entries were dang hard to judge. You folks have sure upped your game. So a big shout-out to all the contestants for giving us some real trouble. However, the results are in and the orange ribbon goes to—" Dodge paused for effect. "Amanda Fittswater."

There was a roar of applause as she marched up to Blake to retrieve her ribbon.

Every time he saw Amanda, whether she was behind the counter at Holey Rollers or he was passing her on the street, she always seemed to be a little too friendly. Today was no exception with her wide smile and the way her hand lingered on his a moment longer than it needed to as he handed her the ribbon.

"Thanks, Doc," she said. "Come on over to Holey Rollers this Sunday and I'll give you a couple free jelly doughnuts on the house, with extra sprinkles."

Then she twisted a curl of her hair and winked.

"Amanda, you're a little vixen, and if I didn't know better, I'd think you were flirting with me."

"I am flirting with you."

"I'm going to tell your mother."

"She flirts with you more than I do." And she grabbed the mic, said a quick "thank you, everybody," took the ribbon and sashayed off to her seat while Maggie threw him a look that said exactly what she thought of the entire exchange…*You're such a cad.*

Blake just shrugged.

Dodge said, "So as not to rile anybody's feathers, will Phyllis Gabaur and Kitty Sullivan come on up, please."

"Kitty's not here, Dodge, but her sister Maggie is," Esther yelled from the front row as Phyllis rushed by her in a flurry of self-assured confidence. Blake wasn't sure what the heck Dodge was doing, but he figured his father had some sort of plan.

"Then come on up, Maggie. We got some good news for that sister of yours."

Maggie hesitantly stepped forward, almost as if she didn't believe it. Her sister, Kitty—the woman who used tofu like a spice—had won a ribbon?

Impossible.

Once the two women were standing next to each other, and Blake was ready to hand the yellow ribbon to Maggie, and Phyllis already had her hands on the blue one, Dodge said, "That there blue ribbon and first prize goes to Kitty Sullivan, and the yellow ribbon goes to you, Phyllis."

The entire audience stood to applaud, but Phyllis refused to let go of the blue ribbon. Instead, she and Dodge got into a small tug of war with it. "Let this here ribbon go, Phyllis."

But Phyllis held on, pulling it toward her with all her might.

When it slipped out of his hands, Phyllis took off like a banshee, yelling, "It's rigged. This is mine and nobody's going to take it from me. Nobody! You hear me? Nobody!"

And off she went into the hot sunny afternoon, blue ribbon fluttering in her hand, floral ankle-length dress whipping around her legs, gray hair wild in the breeze.

"Well, don't that beat all," Dodge muttered, as he and everyone else watched her stumble through the crowd, clutching her ribbon and warning anyone who blocked her escape.

"And there goes Kitty's one and only blue ribbon," Maggie told Blake. "She would've been so proud."

"Nobody would blame you if you tackled Phyllis and wrestled your sister's ribbon out of her hands." Blake had a nice mental vision of that going on in his head.

"She looks mean."

"Blue ribbons hold a lot of clout in this town."

"Apparently, more than I'd ever imagined."

Blake leaned in closer as everyone continued to stare at Phyllis, bounding through the thick crowd. "I know where she lives."

"Does that mean we'll be paying Phyllis a visit?"

"We'd have to steal it."

She turned to him, as if they were discussing something she didn't want anyone else to hear. "Count me in. I've always wanted to play on the dark side of the law."

Blake stared at her, wanting desperately to take her in his arms and kiss her. "I knew you were trouble the first time I saw you."

She tilted her head, and grinned. "Then why'd you hire me?"

Blake felt a rush of heat. Darned if he didn't want her even more. He wondered what she would do if he simply pulled her in close and kissed her. "Crazy, I guess."

"Me, too." And she laughed, leaning into him to bump her shoulder against his.

That simple opening he'd been hoping for. If there weren't a whole mess of people standing around, he'd make use of the moment. Instead, he slid his hand down her back, reached around her tiny waist and brought her in tighter so their hips touched. He desperately wanted to swing her around to kiss him, but he let her go, wiped his brow, and repositioned his hat.

Her phone played some kind of tune. She pulled it from her jeans pocket and stared at it, obviously deciding whether or not to answer it. "Excuse me. I have to take this," she said and walked off to find some privacy.

Hold on, boy, he told himself, as he watched her speaking into her phone. This was neither the time nor the place to be making his move. Besides, he didn't want anything to spook this city filly. He needed to play it just right if he was going to have a chance at winning her heart, which he had every intention of doing.

Miss Russet—an exuberant teenager with blond hair and a bright smile, wearing white shorts, a plaid red shirt, white cowboy boots and a rhinestone tiara— spooned up a mound of mashed potatoes from the pit that had been filled courtesy of a cement truck from Cast in Stone, the local concrete company. The mashers had been poured out of a long metal tube directly into the pit, causing the entire area to smell like baked potatoes. The crowd seated in the eight rows of metal bleachers that ran to the right of Miss Russet roared as she cautiously tasted the potato slush and gave it a thumbs-up.

Maggie's stomach was in knots at the entire concept. However, she did have a serious purpose for being there: to win the coveted Spudphy in the Spud Tug. And dang it, she wanted to win more than almost anything else in the whole world.

She couldn't believe she'd just admitted that.

The rope they would be using for this contest of

will and determination lay coiled like a snake next to the potato pit on the bleacher side. Blake and his two equally good-looking brothers busied themselves with uncurling the monster rope and stringing it alongside the creamy concoction.

"Look at those guys. Most of the single women in this crowd would do just about anything if any one of them even looked her way," Nurse Cori said. She was part of Blake's team.

"Why all the fuss over the Grangers? There seem to be plenty of eligible men at this fair."

Cori turned to her. "Yeah, but most of them don't live in Briggs and the ones who do don't have the reputation the Granger boys have."

"And what's that?"

She eyed Maggie assessingly. "Have you kissed him yet?"

Maggie didn't particularly want to answer that. "I, um, well…"

Cori leaned in like a conspirator. "I mean, have you really kissed him?"

"Not like that, I guess."

"Honey, there's no guessing involved. When a Granger kisses you, you'll know it. Believe me, you'll never forget it." She gazed over at the three brothers and for a split second, her face said it all.

Maggie assumed that, at one time, there must've been a sincere relationship between Cori and Doc Blake that smoldered no matter what path each of them took. Those burning embers would never be completely out…at least not for Cori.

"I'm just passing through," Maggie said. "I can't get involved. Besides, I just got a terrific job offer earlier today. It's with Technix, in their marketing department. It's a good solid company and the benefits are amazing. It's a fabulous opportunity and I'd be silly to pass it up." As soon as she'd said the words, she wished she could take them back. But now the cat was out of the bag, so to speak.

Cori turned to her. "Have you told Doc yet?"

"No. I just received the offer about an hour ago. Not sure how to handle it, what with my sister needing me another couple of months, at least."

"Kitty's resourceful. She'll sort something out. She could move and live with Tim's parents. When do they want you to start?"

"That's just it. Before the end of the month."

"Wow, that's less than two weeks. What did you tell them?"

Maggie hesitated, still confused over her response to the HR department. "That I would let them know in a few days."

Cori smiled. "Briggs is growing on you."

"No...I mean, it's a nice town and all, but I could never—"

"It's Doc, isn't it? You're falling for that cowboy, aren't you?"

"Don't be ridiculous. My sister needs me and I—"

Doc's voice stopped her from finishing the sentence. "Don't just stand there, you two, come on over and help."

"Please don't tell him," Maggie pleaded, as they walked toward Doc. "I'd like to tell my sister first."

Cori shook her head. "Honey, you're in a real bind, and I sure wouldn't want to be caught in there with you for anything. I won't say a word."

"Thanks," Maggie told her, and the two women joined the Spud Tug preparations.

"YOU GUYS ARE TOAST," Helen the barmaid teased, as she helped yank the thick rope over to her side of the pit. Helen's team consisted of three guys and two women, some of whom Maggie recognized from Belly Up.

"Tell me about it when you're covered in bakers," Colt called out to her, teasing right back.

Maggie caught the playfulness in Helen's eyes as she watched Helen taunt Colt. "I'll remind you about this conversation when I hose you off afterward."

"Like that would ever happen," Blake countered.

"You boys are in for it now," Helen taunted, but her eyes never left Colt.

"She sounds determined to win," Maggie whispered in Blake's direction as they worked the rope.

"Don't worry about a thing. You're not going in," Blake assured her, adjusting his hold of the rope. The overwhelming smell of mashed potatoes wafted up from the pit, causing Maggie to second-guess her desire for a Spudphy.

"Here," Blake said, handing her the rope, which made her first in line with him right behind her.

"Oh, no. Not going to happen." She dropped the rope. "Somebody else needs to be first. You or one of your brothers."

"You're the new kid. The new kid always goes first."

He picked up the rope and offered it to her.

"Shouldn't that mean you boys want to shelter me from a potentially nasty potato experience?"

Blake adjusted his hat and grinned. "Not in these parts. Being new means you get the short stick by default. But, like I said, you won't be going in. We've won this event three years running. The Granger team's a team to be reckoned with."

Somebody blew a whistle, and everyone on the team lined up behind Blake, with Dodge bringing up the rear.

Maggie reluctantly took the rope, and faced the other team. She was not happy standing that close to the potato abyss. The only comfort she took in all of this was the fact that Helen was first in line on the opposing team, and part of her would love to see her covered in mashers.

"We can do this," Dodge yelled, trying to rev up the group's morale. Whoops and whistles rose in support, until Maggie spotted the big cowboy from Belly Up grabbing hold of the end of the rope for the opposing team. Suddenly, the pit seemed deeper than Maggie had first thought, almost one-and-a-half-feet deeper. And longer. She felt certain her entire team could fall in and be swallowed up.

"Who's that?" Maggie asked Blake as she nodded toward the big guy at the end of the opposing team's rope.

"Uh-oh," Colt warned.

"That's Milo Gump. Helen's cousin. The man protects her like a mama bear," Travis said, not sounding too happy about their latest enemy.

Maggie gazed over the expanse of the pit and caught Milo's attention. He grinned back at her and shook his head.

"I think I need to move farther back in line," Maggie said.

"On your mark," a man in a bright yellow shirt yelled.

The crowd cheered.

"Too late," Blake said. "Just pull with everything you've got."

"I don't 'got' enough!"

"Get set," the man yelled.

Chants and catcalls from the stands filled the air.

"I don't want to do this!" Maggie pleaded.

"Go!"

"Nooo!" Maggie screamed as the rope tensed and she pulled with everything she had in her.

For a good long minute, nothing happened. No movement from either team.

"Pull," Dodge yelled, and the team took a step back, while Helen's team teetered on the brink of the potato pit.

A momentary rush of adrenaline and triumph surged through Maggie. The Spudphy seemed within reach. She could hear Scout screaming from the bleachers. "Pull Daddy! Pull Maggie!"

Maggie pulled harder.

The rope tensed again. No movement.

"You're comin' down!" Maggie, feeling all confident and cocky, hollered to the other team.

Doc and everyone else on the team whooped with excitement.

Then the audience hushed as Milo's loud grunts echoed across the potato crater. Maggie suddenly felt herself sliding forward. She pulled and pulled, but nothing could stop her movement toward the edge of the potato abyss.

"Hang on," Blake ordered. She felt his warm breath

on the back of her neck, giving her a tiny shiver to know he was that close.

"You hang on…to me. If I go down, you're coming with me," Maggie warned.

"Not today, sweetheart," he bellowed. "This here's a brand-new hat."

Maggie felt herself losing her grip, losing her stance, losing her composure.

"I could be bathing in potatoes and you're worried about your hat?"

"Priorities," he said just as Maggie's feet slid out from under her and she heard herself scream "Oh, my g—"

The next moment her mouth filled with chunky mashed potatoes and everything went black as she struggled to push herself up to her knees in the thick white goo. She'd done a bellyflop right into the middle of the pit. Breathing seemed to be all-important as she flipped herself over, spit out the contents of her mouth and sat in the pool of swirling mashed potatoes, taking in great gulps of air.

The people in the stands howled with laughter as she wiped globs of sticky potatoes off her eyes and nose.

Total mortification curled in her stomach, or was that the onset of nausea? She couldn't be sure.

All she knew for certain was that she wanted to get out of there, fast.

"Are you all right?" Doc Blake asked from somewhere in the darkness. The crowd was still laughing.

"I'm fine," she garbled, still spitting out the last bits of potato.

When she was finally able to see, she stared up at Blake as he stood at the edge of the pit, looking all proud and full of himself. "What a match!" he said, grinning.

"You people are nuts," Maggie told him, brushing her dripping hair off her potato-covered face.

"Yeah, but we know how to have fun."

"Tell me how this is fun?" she shot back, looking out through a tangle of potato stuck in her hair.

"Now, don't be getting into a lather. Nobody knew Milo would be on the other end of that rope."

Blake offered her his hand to help haul her out of the potato mash.

"But once you knew, you still put me first?"

His face lit up with mischief. "An oversight."

"So, I'm an oversight?"

He shrugged, grinning. "You look good in potato. Now, come on, and let's get you out of there."

He leaned over a bit farther, extending his hand.

She stared up at him again, this time not wanting to move, not wanting to think about how she was going to get all this smelly goop off her body and out of her hair.

Then she took his hand, and something came over her. Maybe it was the continuous laughter from the crowd, or the feel of potato between her fingers and down the front of her T-shirt. Whatever it was, she grabbed his hand, and instead of allowing him to help her up, she pulled him down, hard and fast. He tumbled in right next to her.

As he fell forward a look of pure surprise replaced the snarky smirk on his face. "You little—"

But he never had the opportunity to finish the sentence. As he fell, Maggie leaned to her right and he brushed by her, doing a perfect bellyflop in the potato pit.

The audience roared with laughter. Even his brothers joined in the fun, along with Dodge, who was chuckling so hard he held his belly.

"Oops!" Maggie said when Blake turned toward her, eyes stuck shut due to all the potatoes covering his face. "An oversight, I'm sure."

"This is not over," he said, eyes beginning to open.

"Oh, yes it is," Maggie vowed, and made a grab for his splattered hat. She stuck it on her head, stood up, bowed toward the crowd and trudged from the pit, leaving the town's heartthrob in the middle of the spud tub, with Milo Banks now plowing in after him.

Chapter Nine

Blake couldn't seem to let it go that Maggie had not only the nerve to pull him into the pit, she'd sashayed away from the tug with his new hat, the spunky little filly.

Not that he didn't deserve to be publicly humiliated. After all, he'd deliberately placed her in the worst position on the rope line, and against Milo Gump, no less, whom he'd secretly known was going to participate. And she'd gotten the town folk to applaud her shenanigans with gusto, to boot.

"Dang traitors," Blake said aloud as he pulled his rig into a slot in front of Sammy's Smoke House.

Not only did he have to endure getting hosed off by his brothers, who took great joy in squirting him with the icy water, but he'd had to change in a portable outhouse. Fine for a kid, not so fine for a grown man.

He turned off the engine and stepped out of his truck, thankful that Dodge had thought to bring him a change of clothes or he'd still be drenched from the hose attack.

The smokehouse sat on the edge of town, under a cluster of now-golden aspens that shaded the parking lot from the low-hanging sun. Normally, by six-thirty on any given night, the place was hopping. Not tonight. Not with the fair in full swing. Tonight, except for his brothers, Cori and a few other die-hard patrons, the place was almost deserted, just the way Blake liked it. His group would get special treatment from the staff, and the way he was feeling, he needed it.

He hadn't seen Maggie since that afternoon, and for all he knew, she could be halfway back to California by now, and good riddance.

Except she had his hat.

He swung open the heavy wooden door and immediately spotted the little thief, still wearing his hat, sitting next to Scout, surrounded by the rest of his fickle family, along with Cori and her boys. Maggie turned his way and the moment she spotted him, her face lit up. Blake's heart melted. The woman had a power over him that was strong enough to derail a freight train.

"The man of the hour," Maggie bellowed.

Everyone turned and applauded as he walked up to the long wooden table.

"That was sure some show out there today, big brother," Colt said.

"Never thought I'd ever see you covered in Idaho's finest. I'd'a paid good money to see that, and all I had to do was wait for Maggie here to do us proud," Travis chimed in, gesturing to Maggie.

Travis let out a whoop, and everyone joined in on the fun.

Maggie stood and took a couple of short bows, then she picked up a longneck bottle of beer and held it up for a toast. "To the great equalizer...the Idaho spud."

Dang if Blake didn't feel his face heat up, probably turning some nice shade of beet-red.

Everyone clinked glasses and bottles, and even the kids made sure they touched all the glasses on the table.

"And here's your hat, Doc," Maggie said, and flung it in his direction with such precision he was astonished at her aim.

He caught it in one hand and immediately set it on his head. "Much obliged, fine lady. You need to rustle up one of your own."

Maggie reached down to the seat next to her and produced a velvety black cowgirl hat, complete with a gold ribbon and a tiny cream feather, and settled it into place. She looked mighty fine. Mighty fine.

"How do I look?" she shouted.

"Like you belong."

A big smile stretched across her face, lighting up her eyes.

"Ooo-ah, you better watch yourself, Maggie," Colt warned. "That man's got trouble written all over him."

"Have you forgotten what happened just this afternoon? If I can handle a pit of potatoes, I can certainly handle your big brother."

"You may have met your match, Doc," Travis called.

"That's yet to be determined," he shouted.

The group hollered and whistled, as Scout slid off her chair and ran over to him. She looked adorable wearing a bright yellow dress. A pretty yellow and pink flower attached to a thin band held her hair off her face, while her favorite pink cowgirl boots adorned her tiny feet. Blake couldn't believe his little tomboy could look so girly.

"Daddy, where were you? We've been waiting here for a really long time," Scout admonished. He knelt as she went in for a hug.

"I was getting all those potatoes off me, sweetpea. But look at you. How'd you get all prettied up like this?"

"Maggie said she bought me this dress and hair band at the fair. Yellow's my favorite color. Maggie wouldn't let anyone spray her with a hose, so Cori took us to her house and she cleaned up there. Dodge said it was okay for me to go home with Cori and Maggie. We had fun. Maggie taught me how to fix my hair. Don't I look pretty, Daddy?"

She twirled. His sweet daughter was about as happy as a puppy with two tails. Her cheeks glowed from the rush of elation. She could barely contain herself.

"You always look pretty, baby."

"Oh, Daddy, you're so silly. I can't always look pretty, especially when I'm all dirty and my hair's messed up."

"Even then, sweetpea. Especially then."

She hugged him tighter and giggled in his ear. He knew this would be one of those moments they would both remember, and he had Maggie Daniels to thank for it.

He looked over at her as Scout slipped from his arms and skipped back to her seat, holding on to the end of her dress, pulling on it as she spun in tight little circles.

Maggie was busy talking and laughing with Colt, oblivious to the moment she had created. At some point during the night he'd have to find a way to thank her for giving him his little girl back.

AFTER AN AMAZING dinner of some of the best barbeque Maggie had ever tasted, along with some fun conversation with the Grangers, the kids and Nurse Cori,

Maggie found herself in the arms of Doc Blake, two-stepping to Luke Bryan's "Country Girl, Shake It For Me."

"Are you sure you haven't done this before?" Doc asked as he twirled Maggie on the dance floor. She wasn't quite sure herself yet, but she could hold her own.

"I may have kicked up my boots a time or two," Maggie teased. The truth was, the last time she had danced on a worn-out wooden floor to the sound of country music, she couldn't have been more than eight years old.

"Darlin', it's as if you've been shakin' it your entire life."

Maggie chucked and stomped her boot heels in time with the music along with everyone else. She was having the time of her life, and it felt better than she could have imagined. She loved to dance, something she rarely got the chance to do. Normally, she was too busy, and her last boyfriend never wanted to do anything other than dinner and the occasional concert. Nor would he have considered dancing to country music. Way too chaotic for him or even for her. She'd forgotten how much she had once enjoyed it. Now, it was as if she had given herself permission to have fun again, embrace everything country, and for a little while, she would hold on tight.

She let out a whoop, as Blake twirled her a couple of times then pulled her in tight against his body. His chest felt oh-so-good up against hers, not to mention his strong thighs, his confident arms.

Reason and a job offer both told her to hold back,

to stop enjoying this man, while her inner voice told her to enjoy the long looks, the warmth…the passion.

"You sure know how to handle a girl in your arms."

His eyes narrowed with tiny creases forming around the edges. She'd never seen him look so striking. "Sweetheart, you ain't seen nothin' yet."

If Maggie could have swooned, she would have. Blake quickly pulled her in closer. She relaxed and bent backward as he spun her around. He sang some of the lyrics to "Country Girl, Shake It for Me" and Maggie joined in on the chorus.

Suddenly, everyone made a circle around them, clapping, whistling and whooping it up as if Maggie and Doc Blake were the main attraction. Even the kids joined in on the fun.

"This is crazy!" Maggie yelled over the drum of the song. "Everybody's watching."

"Just your typical night in Briggs."

They were dancing side by side now, pounding their heels into the floor with the beat. "What if I fall?"

"Impossible," Blake yelled and he waved his hand for everybody to join them. Within seconds, the entire room had joined them on the dance floor, including the waitstaff.

Maggie no longer had time to think about anything but following the sometimes complicated steps, and before long she was laughing and singing along with everyone else. Her entire body tingled with the music as she twirled to each note.

The song ended in a thunder of applause and hoots. Maggie added several of her whistles to the mayhem and the kids instantly wanted lessons.

She collapsed onto the floor, and proceeded to

play whistle teacher to the delight of each child. Scout got the hang of it first and her proud whistles echoed through the restaurant.

"You've created a monster," Blake chided after his daughter went off to teach little Joey, who couldn't seem to get it. Doc had squatted down right next to Maggie, close enough that she could feel the heat of him.

"Anything I can do to make your life easier," she shot back with a sinister smile.

"I'll get you for this."

"Is that a promise?"

"Ms. Daniels, are you flirting with your boss?"

Reality came crashing through with a vengeance. She stood, and the boys sitting in front of her groaned and asked her to stay.

"Sorry, guys, but Scout will have to help you. It's late, and I really have to go home now."

She turned to Blake. He was frowning in confusion. "What's wrong? Are you okay?"

"I'm fine. Just tired, and worried about Kitty. I don't like leaving her alone for too long."

"Mrs. Abernathy's there."

"She goes to bed early," Maggie said, and went off looking for a ride to her car.

MAGGIE HADN'T MEANT to find herself in this situation. She really hadn't planned for the evening to go this way. Sure, she'd needed a ride home after dinner, or at least a ride back to her car at the fairgrounds, but she was feeling a bit tipsy and allowing her to drive hadn't been an option for Doc. He had insisted on driving her home.

The first kiss had simply happened, like a warm breeze on a summer's day. Doc had parked his truck in the gravel driveway, leaned over and kissed Maggie good-night. An easy kiss. One that he might give to a good friend. Nothing personal. Just a kiss, so she'd kissed him back. A light kiss. Nothing personal.

She then opened the door of the cab, and slid out onto the brick sidewalk.

"You're one surprising woman," Doc Blake told her as he followed close behind as they made their way to Kitty's front porch.

The second kiss, the one that was surely about to happen, could have been avoided if Maggie had said good-night—like that time before—while they were still in the truck.

But she hadn't.

"Why's that?" she asked as they walked together in the moonlight. The air felt cool against her face, cool and clean. She liked it.

"Because for someone who's afraid of kids, you sure seem to know how to make them happy. What's your secret?"

So there she was, on Kitty's porch stairs with Doc Blake close at her side.

"I try to remember what it was like when I was a kid, and go from there." They'd reached the front door and she turned to face him.

"I bet you were all about curls and frills." He slowly pulled her toward him. She didn't resist. Then, as if they'd done it a thousand times, he leaned in and gently kissed her neck, once, twice. A shiver cascaded through her. "I was a tomboy..." She sighed, knowing she should stop this. That she needed to stop this.

But she didn't.

He pulled back. "You?"

She nodded, grinning. "I've never admitted this to anyone, but my favorite pair of shoes was my cousin Emma's cowboy boots. They were two sizes too big. I wore them anyway."

He went back to kissing her neck, brushing her hair out of the way with his hands. A rush of heat played on her skin. Her body tingled.

"You're the most fascinating woman I've ever met," he said, then brushed his lips on hers, not really kissing her, just tormenting her with his touch.

She pushed him back a few inches, thinking she was going to end this, right now, before they went any further. That this thing they were toying with couldn't go anywhere. She had a solid job offer at Technix back in California and he lived... His face lit up with a wicked little smile.

She said, "Are you going to kiss me or what?"

He stared at her for a brief moment, the passion in his eyes burning straight through her. "Definitely, yes," he said, and he kissed her, hard, his tongue touching hers, his mouth both soft and hungry against her lips. Tiny quivers sped along her nerve endings, twisting up inside her belly. Never had she been kissed like this. Never had she wanted a man more. She felt light-headed and dizzy with desire.

Maggie wrapped a leg around his as he ran his hand up her thigh and caressed her butt, bringing her in closer. She moved into him, wanting him, wanting him to take her, now, under the stars, on the porch, until there was nothing left of her but the memory of his incredible kiss.

The front door swung open. "Kitty's water broke," Mrs. Abernathy announced in a loud, clear voice.

Maggie's world stopped.

TWENTY MINUTES LATER, Kitty was in a wheelchair being transported through the E.R., with Mrs. Abernathy on one side, and Nurse Cori on the other, while a male nurse rolled the expectant mother toward a private birthing room. Those babies were on their way and this time nothing was going to stop them.

"I'll be right here, Kitty, waiting for Cori to come get me," Maggie told her sister as she trotted next to the moving chair. "Everything's going to be fine."

But Maggie could tell Kitty was on the verge of a complete meltdown as she sucked in quick little breaths, trying with every ounce of concentration she had to remain focused on what she had been taught in all her natural childbirth classes.

"This isn't how I pictured it," Kitty said, blowing air from her puckered lips. "I wanted to be at home... in my little birthing tub...with my family around me... with Tim holding my hand."

Great big tears streamed down her face.

"I know, honey," Maggie's voice caught in her throat. "This is all good, sweetie. You'll see. All good."

Kitty nodded and tried to smile in between tears and short puffs of breath as everyone hurried down the long hallway picking up more nurses and her doctor as they went.

"Give us about fifteen minutes and you should be able to come in," Cori shouted back to Maggie.

"But I want Maggie now," Kitty moaned.

"Let's get you in a bed first, then Maggie can join

you. I promise," Cori said, her voice fading into the mix of other voices.

The entourage turned a corner and vanished, leaving Maggie in the now empty hallway with Blake, who had been on his cell phone for the past five minutes.

Maggie turned to him for support, but he had his back to her while he whispered into his phone. She didn't know where to go or what to do next, so she waited for Blake to disconnect.

Five minutes later he looked over to her, an expression of concern coloring his face.

"What's wrong?" Maggie asked, worried about the answer.

"It's Tim."

Maggie's stomach lurched. There just couldn't be anything wrong with Kitty's husband, there just couldn't. Not now. Not when she was about to deliver their babies. "What? Tell me."

He took a couple steps closer to Maggie. "He's okay. He's been wounded, and he's on his way home."

Maggie covered her face with her hands as she took in a deep breath. Emotion overwhelmed her. She needed to sit down before she fell down.

Blake put an arm around her and escorted her outside. She took in a couple of big gulps of cool night air before she could ask the question. "How bad?"

"We don't know. Apparently, he decided to keep this from Kitty and his family. He didn't want Kitty to get upset, what with her last scare and all. The good news is they released him from the hospital in Boise a few hours ago, and he's on his way here, right now."

"That's good, right? I mean, how bad can he be if the hospital released him?"

"Well, according to Dodge, who got it from Colt, who's flying over to Boise right now to bring him home, he checked himself out before the doctors officially released him."

Blake rubbed Maggie's back as she leaned against him unable to stand on her own. She felt as if she could handle this news so long as she stayed in his arms. "I don't understand. Is Colt a pilot?"

"Both my brothers can fly. Dodge taught them when they were boys. We own a lot of land and it's the easiest way to take care of it. I never had the bug. Give me four wheels any day."

"How long before they get back here?"

"Couple hours, max."

She trembled. "I'm scared, Blake. Scared for the babies, for my sister, and for Tim."

He pulled her in tighter, then stroked her hair, laying down a kiss on the top of her head. "It's going to be fine, you'll see. Kitty's in good hands and Tim's a smart buck. He wouldn't do anything he didn't think he could handle."

Maggie gazed up into his eyes and found all the strength she needed to get through what promised to be a long night.

Then he kissed her. It was a soft, reassuring kiss, and Maggie knew for this instant in time, she wanted to stay right there, wrapped up in Doc Blake's arms.

Chapter Ten

"I can't do this anymore," Kitty moaned as Doctor Guru, a petite Indian woman with a last name that defied pronunciation—thus the Guru—encouraged her to push. The doctor stood at the end of the bed, black hair pulled back in a tight bun, clad in blue scrubs, white latex gloves and a blue mask covering her nose and mouth.

A patient woman, waiting for another new life to take its very first breath.

"Yes, you can," Doctor Guru urged. "You're a strong, determined woman. Now push!"

The small birthing room, where a cesarean could be performed if necessary, echoed with the reassuring sound of the babies' heartbeats.

Nurse Cori stood next to the bed, watching, waiting. She also wore blue scrubs, but with matching blue latex gloves. "Push, honey. Push!"

Kitty tried, but the effort wasn't there. "Noo," she moaned. "I can't."

She had endured several hours of intense labor and now that the babies were about to emerge, her strength had vanished. Plus, the contractions had lost their intensity, which according to Doctor Guru was normal when delivering twins, making it more difficult for Kitty to feel the need to push.

Doctor Guru had warned Maggie that she might have to take the babies with a C-section if this went on too much longer. Kitty adamantly opposed the procedure unless the babies were in distress.

The contraction subsided and Kitty relaxed. Maggie held Kitty's hand and gently stroked her sister's head. "Come on, sis, next time just one big push. You're almost there."

Kitty tensed with another contraction. Both the doctor and nurse urged her to push. Maggie slipped her free hand behind Kitty's back trying to get her to lean forward, but Kitty was simply too weak.

Maggie had so hoped that by now Tim would have arrived, despite the fog that hung over Boise. But Colt couldn't take off when he'd planned to, so she and Blake had decided not to tell Kitty about Tim's journey home, just in case he didn't arrive in time.

Still, Maggie was desperate for something to get Kitty to work harder one more time or Dr. Guru would have no choice but to do an emergency cesarean.

She squeezed her sister's hand. "Look at me, Kitty." Kitty focused on Maggie. Her sister's fatigue was making her appear pale and weak, causing Maggie to want to give up and let the doctor do the cesarean. But she knew Kitty was looking to her older sister for some courage.

So Maggie couldn't give up.

Not yet.

Not without one more try. "I've got something to tell you, sweetie."

Kitty's face was covered in sweat. Her hair clung

to her head in little tufts. Her nose was crimson from crying. Maggie's heart broke just looking at her.

"What?" Kitty whimpered.

"You're the most beautiful woman in the entire world," Tim's voice echoed from behind Maggie. "And I love you, babe."

Maggie turned to see Tim, leaning on crutches, one leg partially wrapped, a blue support shoe on his foot. Nevertheless, he looked as handsome as ever with his sandy-colored hair, sparkling blue eyes and a smile that could light up the world. At once Maggie was so full of love for her sister, for Tim, the babies and for Blake, who was guiding Tim closer to Kitty's bed.

Kitty squealed and lunged forward, causing the doctor and Cori to immediately respond by easing Kitty back into delivery position.

Emotion swept over Maggie and she couldn't hold back the tears as Tim and Kitty gently kissed and held on to each other, whispering words of love. And just as they did, another contraction rocked Kitty's body. This time, with Tim by her side, she was able to push with every last ounce of strength she had.

"Come on, babe," Tim coached, "I'm right here with you." And within seconds, their sweet baby girl slipped into the world, fussing and cooing. The room ignited with cheers and love as tiny arms reached for the sky. The doctor placed the first baby on her mama's tummy, and Kitty stroked her head, telling her how much she loved her and how happy she was to see her.

Then Cori and Dr. Guru made it possible for Tim to cut the umbilical cord, which he did, as tears stained his face.

Cori placed the sweet baby girl in a small blanket

and handed her to another nurse, who then cleaned her and tended to the severed umbilical cord.

Within five minutes, their son was born healthy and screaming at the top of his lungs. Tim was exactly what Kitty needed to help bring their precious children into the world, and from the way Tim looked, Kitty and those glorious babies happened to be exactly what Tim needed, too.

MAGGIE SAT NEXT TO Blake in the cab of his truck, feeling completely drained. She didn't know if she could move when he finally parked in front of his ranch house. Her entire body felt as if it were made of lead. If she was this tired, this emotionally whipped, she couldn't begin to imagine what Kitty and Tim must be going through.

Tim had been truly incredible with Kitty, even with his injuries. Blake had told her that Tim had sustained some nerve damage in his right leg, but the doctors said he'd be fine with physical treatment. It was just going to take some time, and the one thing that he and Kitty had was plenty of time.

Maggie yawned, a big double yawn that caused her eyes to water and her mind to want to shut down for several days. She'd been awake, with the exception of a few catnaps on a hardbacked chair at the hospital, for almost twenty-four hours. The stress was definitely taking its toll.

Still, all the emotions she had powered through only made her want Blake's arms around her more. Especially now, when she thought of sleeping. She couldn't think of anything more comforting than to be in his arms when she closed her eyes.

"Let's get you to bed," Blake said, pulling the key out of the ignition. The old truck gave a few pings then quieted. She could hear herself breathe.

"Excuse me?" Maggie teased, knowing exactly what he meant, but she couldn't let the opportunity pass.

"You know I didn't mean it that way."

"Ever?"

He adjusted his hat on his head. "You're making this difficult."

"It's fun to see you squirm."

They exited the truck, giving the doors a good slam shut. The sound echoed through the otherwise silent valley, causing night critters to scamper through the dry grass and leaves. Maggie marveled at all she could hear in this tranquil haven, even the rustle of the slight breeze as it rushed past her.

Blake didn't turn back to lock the truck, a detail Maggie truly appreciated about living in a small town.

He sidled up next to her as they headed toward the house, each wrapping an arm around the other's waist. "Just not tonight, darlin.' I think we're both spent."

Dawn peeked over the mountains as Maggie stumbled along. Her feet didn't seem to want to cooperate. He held her closer, hip to hip. They walked in unison.

"You might be right," she said, as another yawn emerged. This time she tried to control it, but she could barely keep her eyes open. Making love to Blake was something she wanted to participate in, and participation in anything but sleep seemed doubtful.

"We've got a comfortable guest room all set up. The bathroom's right across the hall." They continued up the porch stairs, and Blake opened the front door. No need for a key here either. "I'll get you a pair of my pajamas. You might be more comfortable."

Maggie nodded, too tired to speak.

He led her through the dark house, their boots in sync on the wooden floor, then along a short hallway to what had to be the guest room.

Blake flipped the light switch on the wall next to the door. The lamp on the nightstand illuminated the room with a soft glow, giving off a warm ambiance. The walls were painted burnt orange and rustic wooden furniture dominated the small space. Cozy.

"I'll get those pajamas," Blake said, but Maggie didn't hear him. Her full attention was on that comfy-looking bed.

That big, ever-so-inviting bed.

Blake left the room as Maggie slipped out of her boots, letting them fall where they would. Then she unfastened her belt, slid her jeans down, stepped out of each leg, threw the covers back, got in and nestled deep under the covers.

Somewhere in the distance she heard Blake say something, but Maggie couldn't seem to focus on anything but the image of those cute little babies.

She felt Blake kiss her forehead and pull the covers over her shoulders. "Sleep well, sweetheart."

She forced her lips into a smile, and the next thing she knew, sunshine danced on her face and a phone chirped somewhere off in the distance.

MAGGIE ROLLED OVER on her back and slowly opened her eyes, squinting in the bright light at a beamed ceiling she didn't recognize. In her semi-dream state, she tried to recall where she'd seen that ceiling before, but nothing came to mind.

Completely disoriented, she shifted onto her side and focused on the view. The rolling hills in the distance were bathed in a golden orange color that reflected the sun, while the nearby trees played with the breeze. She felt completely content. It was an unusual feeling, one she hadn't experienced often.

Her phone chirped again, and she realized it was signaling the battery was dying. A situation she couldn't easily remedy without leaving the warm bed.

She decided to ignore it.

Just then, a cowboy on a majestic chestnut-colored horse with a creamy mane trotted by. Immediately, she recognized Blake's brother, Colt, the pilot.

Memory of the previous night came rushing in as her dreamy state disappeared: Kitty, Tim, those beautiful tiny babies and Blake Granger. The memory of Blake caused her to quickly check to see if she was naked. To her relief, she still wore the boy-short panties, bra and long T-shirt she'd worn the night before. The only thing missing were her jeans, which she spotted at the foot of her bed.

Not that she didn't long to be naked with Blake, but at the moment the last thing she needed was any sort of added confusion over a sexual tryst with him. She would be leaving soon, and she didn't want any lingering doubts when she drove off to her new job.

She scooted down under the covers and reveled in how peaceful she felt lying in the Granger guest room, and how quiet it was.

Blissfully quiet.

She let out a soft moan, pulled the covers in tight

and thought about how sweet it would be to doze for a few more hours. Sure, she wanted to check on Kitty and the babies, and talk to Tim, but right now all she really wanted was more blissful, uninterrupted sleep.

Her phone chirped again just as there was a soft knock at the door.

"Just a minute," she called, thinking it must be Blake coming to wake her, possibly tempt her with a morning kiss.

Without hesitation she sat up, ran a hand through her tangled hair, tried to get the makeup out of the corners of her eyes, and straightened her T-shirt, which had slipped up her back. She couldn't wait to see him.

Of course, she should be scolding herself. It would be easier on everyone if they didn't pursue their attraction for one another. After all, she had an actual job offer on the table that she was absolutely planning on accepting just as soon as she charged up her phone.

But still…

"Come in," Maggie said, not wanting to move from her little cocoon.

The door burst open. Maggie's eyes went wide as without warning Scout, the two dogs and Colt's three boys raced into the room, jumping up on the bed in a flurry of excited glee.

Not having time to think, Maggie braced herself for the onslaught, wondering if there was some mistake. Perhaps they thought Blake was in this room, or some other guest who was much more fun.

The entire crew spoke at once, even the dogs.

"Maggie! Maggie! You're awake!"

"We've been knocking and knocking."

"Can you play with us?"

As if they'd been trained, the dogs scampered and barked on cue.

"We've been waiting and waiting!"

"What do Kitty's babies look like?"

"Are they all wrinkly? Do you have pictures?"

"When can we see them?"

"Are you hungry? We had flapjacks."

She tried desperately to think of answers to the barrage of questions, all the while being licked by the overly affectionate dogs, but none of her efforts seemed to be working. So, instead, the only thing she could think to do was wrestle Scout down on the bed and start tickling her. Something Maggie had loved when she was a kid.

"Noo," Scout screamed. The boys joined in, and suddenly everybody was tickling everybody and laughing uncontrollably. The dogs kept stepping over Maggie, licking her face and arms, barking.

Complete chaos ensued, and all that peacefulness Maggie had so enjoyed was replaced with the raucous joy of exuberant children and dogs.

"You guys are in for it now," Maggie announced with a flourish, as she playfully whacked little Joey with a pillow.

"Hey, that's my brother," Gavin shouted.

"So, whatcha' gonna do about it, huh?" Maggie teased.

"This," Gavin warned, and bonked her with a pillow, causing her to lose her balance on the edge of the bed, and slip onto the floor with a heavy thud.

Everyone stopped laughing. Even the dogs stopped barking. Maggie could hear soft gasps, as each of the kids realized she was on the floor.

She wasn't the least bit hurt, but she played into their apprehensions as she lay in a snarl of bedding, completely still, eyes closed, mouth tight.

"Is she dead?" Joey asked after a moment. "Did you kill her, Gavin?"

Silence.

Maggie could feel the sheets being tugged, then the dogs jumped off the bed and started licking her face.

That did it.

She opened her eyes. "You guys are in for it now," she yelled, jumping back on the bed.

They screamed and armed themselves with pillows, and laughter reigned. Maggie attacked each of them with more tickling and pillow bonking, as the dogs leaped for her attention.

All Maggie could think of during this madness was how much she loved these little guys. An emotion she once thought would be difficult for her to ever feel for any child, let alone for six of them, Kitty's babies included. As she beat these rascals off with a pillow, she realized she'd been purposely keeping away from kids out of misplaced fear. Now that she was learning how to talk to them, and interact with them, she found that her heart was changing for the better.

Blake was just coming in from helping Colt and Travis oversee the potato harvest when he heard a thump coming from the guest bedroom. Thinking the worst, he ran to see what had happened, only to find Maggie playing on the bed with the kids. The sight of her surrounded by four kids, all laughing uncontrollably, with Suzie and Mush joining in the fun, took his breath away.

He leaned on the doorjamb, tilted his hat back and

marveled at the spectacle. If he hadn't been watching it with his own eyes, he never would have believed it possible. What a difference from her first day on the job when she tried to resign because of the Nezbeth boys, too scared to walk into the office, a look of fear on her pretty face.

Well, she didn't seem scared now, and she appeared to be loving every crazy minute of the pillow fight. He knew the kids could go on like this for hours, an adult wore out in no time flat. He could already see that Maggie was beginning to tire. She was lying down on the bed while the kids tickled her relentlessly. He clapped his hands together to get everyone's attention. "Okay, you guys. Let's give Maggie a break."

The dogs jumped off the bed and raced toward him for some loving. Blake obliged, giving them each a good scratch under their ears. Then he commanded them to sit and stay, which they did.

The kids were calming down, but not enough. They still had Maggie pinned down. "It's time for you all to wash up and get some lunch if you want to see Kitty's babies."

That got them moving. Scout jumped off the bed in a flash, followed by the boys, who raced past him, shouting out their order for sink privileges.

Maggie, in the meantime, lay there like a tattered rag doll that had been over-loved. A great big smile lingered on her beautiful face.

Blake walked over to her, sat down on the bed, and carefully slid her hair back.

"Good morning," he said with a chuckle.

"Is it still morning?"

"Not exactly." He glanced at his watch. "It's closer to midafternoon than morning."

"It's this room. Way too quiet."

"Country life, sweetheart. No cars, no trains and not many people."

"I could get used to this."

"Don't tease me."

She grinned up at him, her cheeks rosy from playing. "Are they always like this?"

"Pretty much." He still held a lock of her hair between his fingers, wanting that connection.

"And do they wake up most of your houseguests this way?"

He let her hair slip from his fingers, and brushed his hand down her bare arm. She felt all warm and silky.

"Depends on the houseguest."

She wrapped her body around him, legs touching his lower back with her head resting on his shoulder. Again, he slid her shiny locks off her face, his fingers tangling up in her hair. If they kept this up, he wouldn't be able to resist her much longer.

She looked up at him, wide-eyed. "I take it I'm acceptable."

"I'd say you're more than acceptable. You've made it to one of the family."

"I think I like that. I like that a lot." Her eyes watered with emotion as a slow wide smile spread across her face. "I've been living on my own for so long I'd forgotten what it's like to be part of a family. Kitty and I had it for a little while when we were kids, before our dad left, then again when we lived with our mom's sister and her husband in Indiana. But once our mom brought us back to live with her in San Jose, everything changed. We hardly saw her because she worked all the time. Kitty spent most of her nights and weekends with friends, while I put in extra time at school to get straight A's. At eighteen I went off to college, graduated with honors, and I've been climbing the ladder ever since. It's a nice feeling to be in a family again. Thanks."

She moved back to her pillow. He leaned over and gently kissed her, their tongues meeting and sending a jolt of desire directly to his groin. She tasted as sweet as a ripe peach. He wanted to take her clothes off and slip into bed with her, stay there all day making love, talking love, savoring her warmth…except he knew better. With four kids, two dogs, two brothers and a cantankerous father in the house, Blake had no choice but to pull back before he couldn't stop himself.

At the moment, lunch seemed like the smarter idea.

Chapter Eleven

Thirty minutes later, after Maggie had showered and gotten dressed in the same clothes, with the exception of one of Blake's black T-shirts, she sat at the kitchen table while Dodge fed her real food. Nothing "healthy" allowed. It was Saturday and Maggie was glad she could take her time and let the day unfold.

Maggie piled her plate with a little of everything that was served and dug in. The food looked incredible and she couldn't wait to take her first bite. She was starving.

"You're as lean as a desert grasshopper," Dodge told her, "but you can eat like a cowpoke that's been out on the trail all day."

"Only when I'm served food like this," Maggie answered. "This is delicious, Dodge. Thanks."

She relished the smells and sights before her, feeling as though Dodge had gone way over the top trying to please her. He had prepared breakfast for a second time especially for her, and the kids wanted more of the same. Besides Dodge's standard lunch fare of baked beans, fried potatoes and warm biscuits, he served up a mess of scrambled eggs, a stack of flapjacks and blood-rare flatiron steaks, just the way she liked them.

"Dodge only grills up flatirons for special occasions," Colt said, looking as if he'd fought a tough battle that morning. Both he and Travis had bad hat hair, and their shirts were dusty. Unlike Blake, who looked as if he'd been working in his office all morning. Clearly, they were different types of cowboys.

"Maggie's our special occasion," Buddy announced, looking all proud of himself for saying it.

Dodge said, "Now don't be gettin' all fired up. Them steaks were on sale, so I got me a few. You boys are making more out of this here lunch than it is, even though I gotta say, Maggie's the first girl I seen in a while that has a hearty appetite. It's somethin' a man like me can appreciate." He turned to Maggie. "Can I get you anythin' else?"

Maggie giggled. "No, thanks. I think I have everything I need right in front of me." She was looking straight at Blake when she said it, then wondering if he would catch the underlying meaning. But he didn't seem to notice. He was too busy cutting up Scout's flapjack.

"This tastes amazing, Dodge," Maggie told him. A bite of steak and everything else made it onto her fork, including a bean or two. "I don't think I've ever tasted a steak this good."

Dodge beamed. Maggie knew how much he loved compliments. "Pure Idaho beef, darlin'. Can't get it in California."

Maggie nodded. She'd taken another bite and her mouth was too full to speak.

"Daddy, did you ask her yet?" Scout whispered loud enough for Maggie to hear. "You should ask her now, Daddy. Please ask her now."

"Later, Scout," Blake told her. "Now's not the time."

Maggie put her fork down, swallowed and looked at Blake. "Sure it is. What's up?"

He was sheepish, as if he didn't know exactly how to ask her and Maggie was loving it. She was able to see yet another side of Blake that she hadn't thought possible. It was the uncertain, vulnerable side of the normally confident Doc Blake, and she liked it.

"Here goes. Once a month, during the summer and early fall, Colt and I take these here high-octane rascals to the Spud Drive-In, buy up a mess of burgers and shakes at the concession stand and watch whatever G-rated movie they're playing. It's not glamorous, and sometimes it can get cold out there, especially this late in the season, but we bundle up tight under the blankets to stay warm. Anyway, the kids wanted me to ask if you'd like to join us tonight. It's a double feature."

All eyes were on Maggie, and without a moment's hesitation she said, "I haven't been to a drive-in since I was a kid. It sounds like fun."

"Does that mean you'll come?" Buddy asked.

Maggie nodded. "Yes, that means I'd love to join you."

The kids whistled and cheered.

"Settle down and finish your lunch," Dodge ordered.

Colt spoke up. "Now that Maggie's going, there won't be much room in that truck bed for me, so I'll take a rain check on tonight if that's okay. I've got something to do, and was hoping you'd be amenable to taking the kids yourself…but now that Maggie's with you, there should be no problem."

Blake addressed him. "Now just hold on, I—"

"That's fine," Maggie interrupted before Blake

could offer his rebuttal. She owed Colt so much for flying in Tim, this was the least she could do. "We can handle it."

For some odd reason, Maggie felt very sure of herself. As if handling a mess of kids at a drive-in was as simple as pie.

Blake shook his head. "I don't know what's gotten into you, Maggie Daniels. Whatever it is, it sure fits in with this family."

"Thanks," Maggie told him as she knocked off the last bite of her scrumptious steak, and contemplated having seconds. "I'd like to stop off at Kitty's place to pick up a few things." She wanted a change of clothes, makeup and her much-needed phone charger. She hated not having a working phone. Not being able to easily access her email, get her messages or receive a text. It made her feel totally disconnected from the real world.

Not that Briggs wasn't the real world, it just wasn't her world, at least not the way Kitty thought of it.

"Good idea." He turned to the kids. "It's a full afternoon, and we better get cracking. If you all are finished, clean up and collect everything you need for the drive-in 'cause we're not coming back."

Scout hopped off her chair and went over to Blake. "I told you she'd come with us. She likes us. I can tell."

Then she ran over to Maggie for a quick hug.

Emotion caught in Maggie's throat. Never had she felt so accepted by a group of people who up until a few weeks ago, she'd only heard of through Kitty. Maggie finally understood why her sister loved this town and these people so much.

Travis stood, took his empty plate to the sink and said, "I best be getting back to it." He slipped his hat on his head, gave it an adjustment and said, "You folks have a nice time."

To Maggie, he tipped his hat then walked out, his work gloves in hand.

Travis seemed like such a nice man, a true gentleman.

When she thought of how temporary this was, sadness overwhelmed her. Now that Kitty's babies had arrived, Tim was home, and his great-aunt, Esther Abernathy, had everything under control, and she knew that Doc could hire almost anyone to take over the office responsibilities, it was time for Maggie to make the call. She had to accept that new job at Technix before they offered it to someone else. And her leaving became impossible.

If it hadn't already.

As soon as she thought of not leaving, and not accepting the offer, a deep shiver passed through her. She quickly dismissed it, claiming it had nothing to do with her thoughts. Rather, with the fact that she'd felt a genuine chill. She gulped her hot coffee, anticipating its warmth as she listened to the boys tell her what she needed to take to Spud Drive-In.

LOADING THE KIDS into the truck took longer than Maggie had expected. An entire hour longer. Once they were at the hospital, they discovered Nurse Cori couldn't let everyone in at once. So each child had individual time with the babies and their proud parents. That was after they scrubbed their hands and put on white masks over their noses and mouths.

"You can't be too careful around newborns," Mrs. Abernathy told them from behind her own mask.

The kids thought it was great fun, pretending to be doctors, but by the time it was Blake and Maggie's turn to visit, it was too late to stop off at Kitty's before the movie to pick up clothes or Maggie's charger. Maggie decided not to fight it and would simply go with the flow. She'd just have to call tomorrow, and she certainly didn't need makeup or have to wear anything fancy for the drive-in.

She and Blake remained in the waiting room with the rest of the kids as one by one each was personally escorted to Kitty's room by Cori, whose enthusiasm for the task never waned. However, Maggie was a nervous wreck. The last thing she wanted was to be forced into holding one of those tiny babies. What if she dropped it or squeezed it too tight or it started to cry? What then? She had no idea how to hold or deal with an upset baby. The whole idea scared her silly. And she definitely didn't want to admit this apprehension to anyone, especially not to Blake, who was as excited as everyone else to cuddle the newborns.

"Kitty's sure going to have her hands full with those two little darlings," Blake said. "Newborn babies are the best. A whole new life just beginning. Sure am looking forward to meeting them. It's like a direct connection to the future. How about you, Maggie? I bet you're chompin' at the bit to get at them."

Maggie attempted a smile, folded her arms in tight across her chest. "Yeah, can't wait."

Blake stared at her for a moment, a warm smile lighting up his face. "Sweetheart, it's going to be fine. I promise. Those babies are going to love you."

He rubbed her back and as crazy as it seemed, she believed him.

Ten minutes later, it was their turn to visit. Mrs. Abernathy was keeping an eye on the kids.

As soon as Maggie entered the private room, she spotted Kitty's stolen blue ribbon attached to a huge bouquet of mixed flowers. Apparently, Phyllis Gabaur had had a change of heart and wanted to spread the love with Kitty, Tim and the babies. By the look of the room, so did everyone else. Outside of a florist's, Maggie had never seen so many flowers, balloons and stuffed toys. It reminded her of how much this town loved Kitty and her family.

Maggie longed to be loved like that and wondered if it could ever happen for her.

"Hi, everyone," Maggie said, as she focused on Kitty sitting up in bed. She'd never looked more beautiful.

"Maggie, you've come!" Kitty said, a look of surprise on her face.

"Of course, you're my sister. Where else would I be?" Maggie leaned over and hugged her sister, looking down at the sweet baby in her arms.

Kitty and Tim each held a baby wrapped in the appropriate-color blanket.

Maggie's first instinct was to run out of the room, but then she reminded herself of her newly acquired backbone.

Maggie stood next to Kitty's bed, peering down at baby Jessica while Blake and Tim greeted each other with handshakes and hugs. Tim said, "I'm glad to see you both made it." He nodded toward Maggie, grinning. "How's she holding up with all those Granger kids?"

"She had a moment, but Maggie's full of surprises."

"Actually, I've discovered I like kids," Maggie announced with all the self-confidence she could muster. She strode over to Tim. "And I'm in need of holding that little boy of yours."

Tim beamed as he handed his new son to Maggie. "This is your Auntie Maggie, Parker." And just like that, with one look, Maggie fell in love with the tiny baby cradled in her arms.

"Look at you," she cooed as Parker squirmed and made a funny face while trying to concentrate on her. "He's the spitting image of you, Tim."

Tim grinned one of those smiles that came from deep in the soul. "He's more handsome than this old cowboy."

"I hope so," Blake teased.

Everyone laughed. Tim's angled face was cover-model perfect, and his body was always in top athletic condition. Even now, while he sat in a chair with his leg propped up on a cushion, Maggie knew in her heart his injury was only a temporary condition. Nothing could keep Tim down when he put his mind to it. That determination had always been a trait Maggie admired in him.

A trait Blake had in spades.

Chapter Twelve

Spud Drive-In was everything the kids had promised it would be. There was even a giant plaster russet potato that sat in the bed of a red pickup truck in front of the massive movie screen.

Naturally, the kids wanted to climb all over it, but Blake discouraged that from happening by driving right past it and backing up into his preferred spot in the tenth row, center, which still happened to be available.

"How did you score this spot? This is perfect," Maggie said.

"We're all pretty much regulars. Everybody respects each other's space."

Maggie had trouble with the concept. "So, you're saying even though other people have arrived ahead of us, no one will take this spot because they know you like it?"

"Pretty much, yeah."

"That's amazing."

"That's a small town."

Clearly, living in a small town had its advantages, but this was way over the top compared to Maggie's competitive world. The last movie she'd seen was at one of those new plush theaters with leather recliners, a wait staff to take your drink and food order, and your own side table to hold all your goodies. Children were better left at home and attire was business casual, a movie theater for the busy trendsetters, not for the laidback Spud Drive-In crowd.

As soon as they'd parked, everyone jumped from the truck to claim a spot in the bed, making sure they each had enough pillows, blankets and room for all the treats they planned on getting. Maggie, too, made a place for herself up against the back of the truck bed with Blake right next to her.

They had barely gotten settled when the previews began. It was going to be a long night: a double feature. The first movie was *Brave,* and the second was *Madagascar 3: Europe's Most Wanted.* Two movies she would never have considered seeing if she was in the Bay Area. But given she was at a drive-in that sported a massive spud as a draw, and had four kids to tend to, she couldn't wait for the opening credits.

When the kids wanted to take off for the concession stand, with Blake trying to keep a lid on their excitement, she decided she was staying put.

"Better come on along, or there's no telling what you'll end up with," Blake warned.

But Maggie didn't want to budge. The blankets, the pillows, the open sky, she didn't want to risk changing one thing for fear of spoiling the moment. This was exactly how she wanted to be. "Popcorn, a burger, fries and a shake will be fine. Besides, somebody has to stay here and watch all this stuff."

Maggie tried for sincere, but she could tell Blake

wasn't buying it. He tilted his head, and gave her a "really?" look.

"C'mon, Uncle Blake, hurry up! I don't want them to run out of anything," Buddy insisted.

Scout pulled on his hand. "She wants to stay, Daddy. It's okay. Let's go. I'm starving."

After they'd gone, Maggie snuggled into the pillows, and stared up at the star-filled sky. She made a wish on the brightest star for many more moments like this, and then focused on the movie screen, totally content.

Could she do this? Could she live like this for the rest of her life? Maybe the reason she hadn't immediately accepted that job offer was because she really wanted to stay right here in Briggs, if Blake would have her.

BLAKE HERDED THE KIDS through the rows of parked cars, making sure each of them had a hand to hold on to.

"Stay together and don't run," he ordered.

Amazingly, they paid attention and walked in a straight line, with Blake in the lead like the Pied Piper. There were several overhead pole lights, and whatever they didn't brighten, the screen took care of. Just enough light to guide them to the concession stand, so everyone could see exactly where they were going.

Spud Drive-In was crowded with locals. Blake nodded, tipped his hat and smiled at anyone he knew, which was most everyone.

But as he walked, keeping one eye on the kids, it occurred to him how completely dumbfounded he was by Maggie's recent change. He'd known from the very first time he'd met her that she had a Country heart, although, he had no idea she'd embrace it so quickly.

Would this change be enough to keep her in Briggs? That was still to be decided. She hadn't mentioned anything about leaving, yet, so he allowed himself to feel somewhat encouraged by her easy willingness to join him and the kids at the drive-in.

He was falling hard for this girl, and no matter how hard he tried to keep reminding himself this hunger for her might never be satisfied, part of him wouldn't let the hope die.

Blake realized he was deep into familiar territory. Hoping for different results with the same type of woman as his ex. Was he truly insane or was his caring for Maggie shadowing reality? Could it be another trap?

Only time would tell. Tonight, anyway, he intended to keep his heart locked up tight. Maggie was merely slumming with country folk. She could act the part, but it was all window dressing. She was a city girl tangled up in a honky-tonk, and would break his heart in a New York minute. The trick was to keep his distance and concentrate on the movies and not that sweet smile of hers, or that smokin' hot body that turned him on with her every move.

"Will this be all for you, Doc?" Milo Gump asked from behind the mound of food on the counter. Blake had gotten so deep into his own thoughts that the kids had gone hog wild with their order.

Scrutinizing the pile of treats, he thought he should put some back, then decided he was too distracted to argue with a pack of hungry kids.

"Um. Yeah, that should do it."

"And then some," Milo chided and began ringing everything up.

Blake shook his head to try to knock some sense into it. After all, he did have four rambunctious kids to think about. This was no time to dwell on his lust for Maggie Daniels, no matter how much he wanted her.

He forced himself to concentrate on the task at hand. It seemed like the boys had ordered everything on the menu, including huckleberry milkshakes, Spud Buds, several orders of spicy fries, extra dipping sauce and double-double cheeseburgers all around. "Our absolute favorite," according to Gavin, who could eat like a truck driver if his dad would let him. Indeed, his favorite food was a basket of Spud Buds, deep-fried tater puffs, with an extra bottle of ketchup mixed with hot sauce. Gavin loved hot spicy food, and would pour hot sauce on cake if he had the chance.

Scout was more into a plain burger, no sauces of any kind, no cheese, regular fries, no ketchup, and a child-sized buttered popcorn.

"So, Doc, I see that city filly is sittin' back there in your rig. Word is she's your new girl. That true, Doc?"

"You know better than to believe the gossip in this town."

The kids didn't seem to hear the conversation. They were too busy trying to figure out how to carry everything to the truck.

"I know better not to, Doc, and so do you. Always somethin' to it, though from the looks of that pretty little thing, she'd fit in your barn just fine."

"She's not staying. She's moving back to the Bay Area in a few weeks."

"When did that ever stop you from tryin'?"

"This time. It stopped me this time."

Milo grinned. "Then what's she doin' in your bed?"

Blake's throat tightened as he coughed. "Where'd you hear that?" he whispered, annoyed. "This town is way too interested in my private business. I don't know why I ever came back here. Can't a cowboy be nice to a woman without everyone thinking they might get together? Okay, sure, I like her just fine, but she's the leaving type and I've already been down that road. I'm not going down it again. I'm surprised at you, Milo, saying such things. Don't you have better things to do than comment on my love life?"

His heart raced and his hands were clenched. He couldn't believe the way people talked in this town, Milo included. He'd always thought Milo was his friend.

"I meant in your truck bed, Doc, not your sleepin' bed."

Immediately, the fight drained out of Blake. He felt so foolish, like his brain needed scrubbing. The kids had gathered up the food and were staring up at him, waiting for his next move.

"Oh." He sighed.

Scout spoke up. "There's no room at Kitty's house since her babies came, so Maggie's staying in our guest bed. Tim came home from the war, and Mrs. Abernathy is sleeping in Kitty's guest bedroom. That's why Maggie's with us. We have lots of room. Besides, Maggie's funny, and she loves drive-in movies so she came with us tonight. My daddy likes her, I can tell."

Blake shuffled his feet. "Now don't be saying things that aren't true."

Scout turned to him, looking all innocent and little. She could melt his heart with one glance. "Don't you like Maggie, Daddy?"

"Sure I like Maggie. Just not the way Milo thinks I like her."

"How does Milo think you like her?"

Blake hesitated. Now was not the time to go into his feelings for Maggie, especially since he wasn't quite sure of them himself. "Um, I can't explain it right now, sweetpea."

She *tsked,* and stuck a hand on her hip. "Why not, Daddy?"

"Because liking someone can be difficult to explain."

Her forehead furrowed. "Either you like somebody or you don't. It's easy. Sometimes you're just downright silly, Daddy."

Both Milo and Blake chuckled, then Milo reached into the glass case and pulled out two boxes of Junior Mints. "On the house, Scout. For you and Maggie."

As Scout squealed her surprise, Milo shook his head. "Sorry, Doc, but there ain't no hope for you against those two."

"There's absolutely nothing going on between Maggie and me. We're friends. Nothing more," Blake protested.

"Uh-huh," Milo said, nodding to the next customer in line.

Blake had no choice but to gather up his hellfire crew and head on back to his truck and Maggie Daniels, who, apparently, everyone in town thought he was sleeping with.

For once the town had it wrong, and Blake was hellbent on keeping it that way.

Chapter Thirteen

The night slipped by without an incident. The kids were too engrossed in the movies to cause any problems. If you asked Maggie, they were downright boring. She had expected turmoil of some kind. But they were perfect little angels, which made her question whether they were acting this way for her benefit, or if they were always this good.

In the meantime, Maggie felt like a kid herself what with all the goodies they'd had, particularly the Junior Mints from Milo, which had been her all-time favorite movie treat when she was a kid. Aside from the few that she shared with Blake, she had consumed the entire box.

"What are your feelings toward large women?" Maggie asked Blake once she'd eaten the last Junior Mint. She wanted to know how shallow he was when it came to a woman's curves.

"Tall or round?" Blake teased.

"Round."

"You could probably use a few pounds. Remember, I've seen the way you eat, and it's not likely that'll be happening with a puny box of Junior Mints."

"You never know. They might be my tipping point."

"Then tip right on over here and let's just see if round makes any difference."

He pulled her in closer, giving her a gentle kiss. "Umm, as sweet as honey. Can I fetch you another box?"

"You'd do that for me?"

"Sweetheart, I'd get you an entire truckload."

He kissed her again, then turned back to the movie screen, a great big smile on his face. Maggie felt a buzz down to her toes.

Looking at him now, while he stroked Joey's hair as he rested his head on Blake's long legs, she knew shallow wasn't part of his DNA. The man was one hundred percent down-home warmth, and if she wanted to be a part of that warmth, she had to leave her city world behind.

Could she really do that? For true love, she thought she could do just about anything. She was sure of it now.

The kids eventually fell asleep, leaving Maggie and Blake cuddled together, sharing the remains of the popcorn. At one point Maggie fell asleep as she, too, rested her head on Blake's chest. She couldn't help it. She hadn't felt that safe ever.

When the second movie finally ended, Blake moved the boys into the cab and Maggie carried Scout, who didn't seem to want to let go. On the way home, Scout remained asleep while sitting securely in Maggie's lap.

First, Blake wanted to drop off the boys at Colt's place, a two-story ranch house about half a mile away from the main house on the town side of the Granger property.

"My boys give you any trouble?" Colt asked in a soft

voice as he and Blake lifted the two youngest from the cab. Buddy was awake enough to walk.

"Not once. They were perfect," Maggie told him.

"I'm lucky. They take after their mamma. She always knew when to kick it up and when to calm it down. My boys seem to know the same difference. It's like there's a part of her in each one."

Maggie noticed a longing on Colt's face as he talked about his wife. She could see that he still loved and missed her.

"I wish I could have met her."

He secured a sleeping Joey in his arms. "You two would've liked each other, Maggie. You're cut from the same cloth."

He then headed for the house, leaving Maggie to wonder why he'd said that. She assumed she'd be as unlike Colt's deceased wife as apple pie is from a skinny latte. What did he see in her that she couldn't see in herself?

The answer eluded her completely.

ONCE SCOUT was tucked in bed, and the house was quiet, Blake took Maggie's hand and walked her to her room. Nothing needed to be said when he led her inside and kissed her with all the intensity of a man on fire.

Maggie moved in closer to him, slipping out of her borrowed jacket, then her sweater, and letting them fall to the floor. She wanted to feel his arms around her. Wanted to feel his lips on hers, wanted to know what it meant to really kiss a Granger.

He pulled back and said, "We probably shouldn't do this, but you're making it hard."

"I hope so," Maggie said with a sly smirk.

He kissed her again, a warm, passionate kiss. Gone was the urgency she'd experienced on Kitty's front porch. This time it was about what they felt rather than what they wanted.

Blake kicked the door shut with just enough force to make it close, then he turned and locked it before he began to pull up her shirt, slipping it over her head and tossing it aside. She kicked off her boots, then he unzipped her jeans and slid them over her hips and slowly down her legs. He knelt and helped her step out of them, then ran his hands up her legs and over her butt as he stood up.

She wore a white lace mini-bra and matching panties, and by the look on Blake's face, she figured he was enjoying her choice.

Moonlight streamed in through the windows, giving everything an ethereal feeling, as if the moon was shining just for them.

"You're beautiful, Maggie. More beautiful than I ever imagined."

She lifted his T-shirt and tugged it over his head, revealing his muscled chest. An intense desire to make love to him roared within her.

"Not so bad yourself, cowboy."

His smile lit up his face as he kicked off his boots.

He pulled a wallet out of his back pocket and tossed it on the nightstand. "There's no getting around it this time, sweetheart."

"No getting around it," she repeated with a wicked lilt to her voice.

"No turning back," he said, as he gently eased her down on the bed. "You're one ornery woman, you know that?"

"So I've been told."

He kissed her again, his hand moving from the side of her face to brush her ear, before stroking her hair.

Maggie paused to wonder if Blake could ever love her the way Tim loved Kitty. If she was meant for that kind of unconditional love, and if he did ever fall in love with her like that, would she be able to love him in return? Would she be able to love deeply, without fear that he would leave her for someone else?

Then she stopped thinking. His kiss deepened, their tongues pressing together, tasting, licking, sending shivers up and down her body. She pulsed with yearning for him and all doubt vanished, replaced with an intense need to love and be loved. Cori had been right, never in her entire adult life had she been kissed like this.

She wanted more from him, much more.

They kept kissing, exploring, lying alongside each other, holding each other so close she could barely breathe.

Somewhere during the past twenty-four hours, watching Tim with Kitty, seeing their babies being born, spending time with Scout and the boys, with Blake, all Maggie's apprehensions had vanished, and what she had left was a human desire to be loved. Truly and deeply loved. The kind of love she once could only dream of. The kind of love she desperately wanted. Needed. Longed for.

They moved together in complete silence, as if they were trying to guard their lovemaking from the rest of the world. Every kiss, every touch brought on an emotion that Maggie had never experienced with any other man. She felt as if she was making love, truly making love, for the very first time.

When they finally shed the rest of their clothes and lay in each other's arms, naked, a fire raged deep within her. A fire that rendered her helpless each time he caressed her body. The need to have him inside her was almost more than she could bear.

"Now," she whispered as he moved on top of her, deliberately taking his time, tormenting her with each touch, then slowly slipping a condom over his firm erection. "I want you now."

When he entered her, he let out a deep groan that seemed to come from his soul. A rush of excitement tingled over her body and she allowed a low, heavy sigh to escape.

"Where have you been all my life?" he whispered.

"Trying to find you," she told him while looking deeply into his eyes.

"I'm right here darlin'. Not going anywhere. I'm in love with you."

A tinge of doubt flitted through her head. Could this be real? Could she trust him? Could she trust herself?

She dismissed the questions. Right now all she wanted was Blake, and nothing else mattered.

"Me, too" slipped from her mouth before she could stop herself.

The intensity of their passion increased with the speed of his movements, and just when she thought she couldn't endure the sensation another second, they shuddered their release together, as if they had planned it to happen this way. She couldn't help but groan out her pleasure, causing Blake to hold on to her even tighter.

Afterward, while he rested on top of her, their breathing slowing to a normal rhythm, she marveled at the power of her passion for him, and the emotions surrounding it.

Then, as she cuddled up next to him, cradled in his strong arms with their legs twined, she cried.

BLAKE AWOKE TO FIND Maggie still wrapped in his arms, facing him. They had barely moved. The clock on the nightstand read a few minutes after nine, and he knew, as much as he wanted to stay right there for the rest of the day, if he didn't slip out of bed right now, Scout and Suzie would be searching for him.

Still, he took a moment to watch Maggie as she slept: the rich black hair swirled around her lovely face, the body—an incredibly beautiful body—draped around his, her breathing even and steady. He felt as if he'd died and gone to cowboy heaven.

He was in love again, or maybe he was in love for the very first time. The feelings he had for Maggie were different, as if he never knew what true love felt like until now. Watching her sleep, he knew he wanted her in his bed every night, and from what she'd said and done, he felt hopeful that she wanted the same. It didn't make sense to him that a woman would make love the way Maggie had if she intended to move on up the road.

He had to know for sure. Had to know now. This minute.

Just as he was about to gently wake Maggie with a kiss, he heard Scout and the dogs running through the hallway outside the bedroom door. At one point, he even thought he heard someone knocking on the door.

Suddenly Maggie stirred, rolled over, then settled up against him, her long legs all mixed up with his.

The warmth of her body caused a desire so intense he could barely control it, but there was nothing he would do about it then. Not with Scout out there on the hunt. He'd have to wait until that night, or later that day if he could get Maggie alone.

Reluctantly, he moved out from under Maggie's grasp, trying his darnedest not to wake her. The past couple of days had been such an emotional time for her, the woman needed all the sleep she could get.

He grabbed his clothes off the floor, slipped everything on as best he could, found his boots under the bed, no time to pull them on, and made his way out of the room, trying to be as quiet as a barn mouse.

As soon as he closed the door behind him, he heard a stranger's voice coming from the kitchen. A female voice sounding official and asking for Maggie Daniels. He didn't know what the woman wanted with Maggie, but her voice made his skin get up and crawl. She certainly wasn't from Briggs.

He stood like a deer in the headlights not knowing which way to go—back into the room to wake Maggie—or into the kitchen to see what this intruder wanted. Either way, he felt like a rabbit in a wolf's mouth.

Before he could get his mind and body in first gear, Scout and Suzie came charging down the hall, boots and paws stomping on the wooden floor, Scout's arms outstretched, Suzie's pink tongue flapping. Both dog and child crashed into him with such force his boots flew out of his hand, heels bouncing off the bedroom door then sliding along the floor.

It took all of Blake's strength to keep himself upright.

"Daddy, oh, Daddy! There's a business lady here asking for Maggie. She said that Mrs. Abernathy told her to come here. But I knocked on the bedroom door, Daddy, and she didn't answer. I've looked everywhere for her, but I can't find her. Do you know where she's hiding? The lady in the kitchen really wants to talk to her. What do you think she wants, Daddy? Is Maggie in trouble?"

"I don't know, Scout. We're just going to have to wait and see."

Suzie kept trying to get at the bedroom door, and Blake kept trying to move her out of the way.

"Why did you sleep in the guest room, Daddy? You're not a guest. Maggie's our guest. That's her bedroom. Yours is upstairs next to mine."

She giggled.

Blake stared down at her, trying to come up with an excuse. "I was tired and didn't feel like walking up the stairs."

"That's silly, Daddy. Nobody gets that tired." She made a big eye roll for emphasis causing Blake to chuckle.

"You're right. Next time no matter how tired I am I'll walk up to my own bedroom. Did the lady tell you her name?"

Scout nodded, all pleased with herself. "Yes. Her name is Ms. Allison Bennett."

"Did she say where she was from?"

She shrugged. "Do you want me to ask her?"

He sank down on one knee, getting her complete attention. Suzie walked around him to scratch on the door.

"No. That's okay, sweetpea. Please tell Ms. Bennett that Maggie will be out in a few minutes."

"I looked everywhere for her, Daddy. She's not here."

"I know where she is."

Suzie began sniffing and whining at the door. Scout hesitated, watching Suzie, then she cocked a hip and stuck a fist to it. "Is Maggie asleep in there? But why didn't you tell me, Daddy? Is it a secret? Doesn't she want to see Ms. Allison Bennett? She looks like a nice business lady, Daddy. Maggie doesn't have to be afraid."

"Scout, you ask far too many questions. Just run along and tell the lady that Maggie will be right out."

"Okay, but I don't think I like this hide-and-seek game. You and Maggie don't play fair."

Scout and Suzie clambered back out to the kitchen.

Blake picked up his boots, turned and opened the door to the guest room. Maggie stood in the middle of the room, partially dressed in the clothes he'd peeled off her. Even though she wore the same jeans and boots, and was trying to pull on his T-shirt, the one she'd worn just last night, she somehow looked entirely different.

Her hair was pulled back tight, like she'd worn it the first day he'd met her. Her cheeks were bright pink, matching her pink glossy lips. The lips he wanted to kiss again and again. Gone was the country girl he'd left in bed, naked, pressed up next to him. In her place was Ms. Maggie Daniels, as citied-up as she could get wearing his shirt and her tight jeans, all ready to meet Allison Bennett...obviously another city girl who probably came to fetch Maggie.

He needed to know why, but whatever it was, he had a strong feeling it wouldn't be good…for him.

His stomach tightened, his mouth went dry and a funny feeling crawled up his spine. "I take it you heard Scout."

She nodded, as she perched herself on the edge of the amber-colored club chair to pull on her boots. "I can't believe that Allison Bennett is here…in Briggs…in your kitchen…asking for me. There has to be some kind of mistake."

Maggie seemed to be as pleased as a little heifer heading for its mama's teat.

"Is this Allison Bennett somebody important?"

She hesitated, as if she was reluctant to give up the details.

"You could say that, yes."

She sounded cold and distant. Like he was someone she didn't have time for.

He pressed on anyway. "Is she a friend of yours?"

"I wish." Maggie stood then let out a sigh as she gazed down at her dirty boots. "In the tech world she has the popularity of a female version of Steve Jobs when he was alive, but she's actually more like the queen of the global communication business. And she's here. Asking for me." She shook her head and stared at Blake. A smile stretched across her lips. "She must be lost, or confused. Maybe she's working for Technix now and wants my decision."

A strange look came over her. A look Blake couldn't quite place. As if she'd just said something she hadn't meant to.

At first, Blake didn't get what she was referring to,

then slowly he understood. Maggie had a job offer in her field and she hadn't told him.

He took a step back. His body tensed. He got it now. Got everything. He felt as if he'd just been sucker-punched. "You warned me the first day I met you that you had other applications out there. Did one of them come through?"

She let out a breath, the smile left her face. "It did."

"And when were you going to tell me?"

He did everything he could to hold back the anger that was brewing inside him. Was their lovemaking her way of saying goodbye?

"I haven't said yes yet."

"What does that mean?" The back of his neck ached. He could barely move it.

She passed him without glancing up. As if she couldn't look him in the eye. "It means I'm still thinking about it."

"Does this Bennett woman have anything to do with that decision?"

She stopped in front of the door, and turned to face him. "No. At least I don't think she does. Allison left a big multinational company six months ago to have a baby. I really don't know why she's here."

"Then she's not just an old friend dropping in to say hello."

Maggie shook her head.

As much as it ripped his insides apart, he said, "You know there were no strings attached to last night. Whatever I said wasn't meant to keep you here if you don't want to stay."

She nodded, her eyes welled up and she stared at

the floor for a whole minute, then, regaining her composure, she said, "I know. Thanks."

She grabbed the brass knob, slowly twisted it and moved out of the room, closing the door behind her.

Blake let out the sigh he'd been holding deep in his lungs and plopped down hard on the bed. "You did it again, Doctor Blake Granger. You're the royal chump once more. Your brothers, Milo, and hell, the whole damn town knew what you couldn't admit. She's a leavin' city girl, and you're a first-class Country moron."

He needed to get out of there. Needed to blow off some steam. Needed to get away from Maggie, and Allison Bennett and all city girls. What he needed most at that moment was pure Country.

Chapter Fourteen

Maggie was a mix of emotions. On the one hand she was thrilled that Allison Bennett had taken the time to find her, but on the other, Allison couldn't have found her at a more confusing point in Maggie's life. Not only was she now totally smitten with Blake, but up until this meeting she was considering making Briggs her home, a concept that just a few weeks ago would have been inconceivable.

As soon as she was outside the kitchen, Scout and Suzie came running toward her.

"Did my Daddy tell you Allison Bennett is here? She's so nice. She has a baby at home in San Francisco. Is she your friend? She'd be a nice friend."

Maggie took Scout's hand. "I don't really know her, Scout, and I don't know why she's here. So could you sit with me when she tells me? I think I'm a little nervous to meet her. She's a very smart lady."

"I bet she's not as smart as you are. You got Tanner to sit in my daddy's dentist chair. Nobody ever did that before. Not even Kitty, and she tried lots of times. You have to be really, really smart to do that."

Maggie stopped, bent over and gave Scout a tight hug.

"Thanks, Scout. I knew I could count on you to say just the right thing."

"Anytime," Scout said, waving a hand as if she did this kind of thing all the time. And from what Maggie knew of Scout, she probably did.

"Here she is," Dodge said, as Maggie and Scout walked into the kitchen.

Allison Bennett was in her mid-thirties, with deep brown hair tied in a long ponytail. Dressed in a black pantsuit and a crisp red blouse, she sat at the kitchen table nursing a mug of steaming coffee. Her black mega-purse sat at her feet next to Mush, who seemed to have a fascination with its smell. Somehow Ms. Bennett didn't quite fit inside this cowboy's house.

She stood when Maggie entered the room and held out a hand, formality radiating from every inch of her.

At once Maggie fell into business mode and took Allison's hand, giving it a good firm shake. "It's so nice to finally meet you, Allison. I've been an admirer of yours for quite some time."

"The feeling's mutual," Allison said.

Maggie almost gasped out loud, but caught herself when Scout gave her hand a tug.

"Thanks," she said confidently. Not that she was feeling the least bit confident. More scared silly than anything else. Still, she knew enough to appear calm and self-assured: never let them see you sweat.

"Coffee?" Dodge asked Maggie.

"Yes, please."

Maggie pulled out a chair across from Allison, and Scout climbed up on her chair at the end of the table. When Dodge set Maggie's coffee in front of her, he turned to Scout. "Let's you and me check the cattle barn so's these here ladies can chat."

"She's okay, Dodge. Thanks. I told her she could stay," Maggie countered.

Scout sat up straighter in her chair, a wide grin spread like sweet honey across her face.

"Only if you're sure. She might be small, but she can pack a wallop when she wants to."

Scout wasn't about to sit back and accept his view of her. "I won't say anything unless someone asks me a question. And I'll say please and thank you, I promise."

"She's fine, Dodge. Really," Maggie told him, throwing Scout a warm nod.

Dodge grabbed his worn cowboy hat off the hook next to the fridge, tipped it to Allison, then settled it on his head. "Been a pleasure, Ms. Bennett. Drop by anytime you're in these parts. Door's always open."

"Thanks," Allison told him as he walked away, through the living room, then out the front door. Mush followed right behind him, his long tail up in the air.

"I hope you didn't have trouble finding the place." Maggie reflected on her first attempts at finding Briggs and how she'd driven past the town several times before she realized what she'd done.

"We have a house over in Jackson, Wyoming. My husband's an avid skier, so we practically live in Jackson during the winter. No trouble finding Briggs. I knew exactly how to get here. The trick was finding you, and if it wasn't for the annual Spud Tug, I may not be here right now. My niece is Miss Russet."

"Your niece is Miss Russet?" Maggie repeated, thinking how unbelievable that seemed.

"Yes," Allison said curtly. "And during her reign, she travels to as many fairs as possible. She told me all about you and how you pushed Doc Granger in the spud mash. You're a hoot on YouTube."

Maggie wanted to crawl under the table. She had no idea somebody posted the Spud Tug. "I'm a hoot?"

"At least in Idaho. That's the thing. Social media picks us up when we least expect it to, and something as innocuous as the local Spud Tug can go viral in a matter of hours. Our mission at Bennett Media is to tap into that viral trend and use it to benefit our clients. Some really good things can happen because of it. Like me being able to find you."

"But you found me because of your niece, Miss Russet."

"She actually prefers *Ms*. Russet. It sounds a bit more professional, don't you agree?"

Maggie wanted to remind her they were talking about a vegetable queen, but she grinned and nodded instead. "Yes, much more professional."

Allison's face suddenly flipped to serious business, not that she had given off any real signs of levity while they were discussing Ms. Russet, or even the Spud Tug, but now she was completely transformed. "I'll get right to the point and not waste any more of your time. I heard that Technix has made you an offer. Is that true?"

"Yes, but how did—"

"It's a small world we travel in. I'll double whatever they've said they'll pay you if you'll consider coming to work for me. I don't know if you've heard the rumors, but let me clarify what's actually going on. I'm in the process of opening my own marketing firm. I'll have an office in Los Angeles and one in San Francisco, and perhaps one more once we get going. I don't know exactly where yet. I'd like you to head the office in Los

Angeles. You're my top pick, but I do have other potential candidates on my list."

She bent over, pulled a black folder out of her purse and handed it to Maggie, who was now trembling on the inside. She reminded herself to breathe as she gazed over at Scout. She seemed transfixed by Allison.

"You'll find all the information you'll need, including a list of clients who have already signed with us, and a cash prospectus of investors along with the financing I have secured. There's also a job description for you, and a very generous compensation and bonus package based on time worked and client satisfaction."

"And when would I have to give you my answer? I hadn't considered working in L.A. What part?"

"Brentwood. I was able to get exactly the look I wanted for that office. I'm sure once you see it, you'll agree that it's an amazing location. Plus, I'm offering you a very generous moving package, with a year's lease on an apartment just a few blocks away. Our first year will be critical and I don't want you having to commute through L.A. traffic. I'm sure you're familiar with the kind of time a person has to put in to make a new company work, so I'll need your full attention."

"I understand," Maggie said while trying desperately to take it all in. She placed the sleek-looking file on the table and noticed that Scout kept rubbing her eyes. Her little face was wet with tears. "Scout, honey, what's wrong?"

"I want my daddy," she said between sobs.

"Sure, sweetheart." Maggie turned to Allison. "Excuse me."

She stood and went over to Scout to give her a reassuring hug, but Scout shrugged her away.

Allison stood. "Can I do anything? Get her anything?" She turned to Scout. "Don't you feel well? I bet it's your tummy. Am I right?"

Scout let out a mournful wail. Then she caught her ragged breath and said, "I don't like you. You're not smart. You're stupid. You're a stupid lady and I hate you. Go away! Go away and never come back."

"Scout," Maggie admonished, completely surprised by Scout's mean outburst.

She reached for Scout, but she jumped off the chair before Maggie could catch her and ran out the front door, with Suzie barking at her heels.

"I'm so sorry," Maggie told Allison. "I don't know what happened. That's so unlike her. She's usually the sweetest girl ever."

Allison slid her purse over her shoulder. "Children are pretty straightforward. She obviously didn't like something I said. I guess Mr. Granger was right about that little spitfire. She'll make a great businesswoman someday."

But Maggie was too upset to focus on anything else Allison might have to say. "Sure," she replied.

"I think I should leave now while you tend to family matters. But please know that I would like an answer within twenty-four hours, and you would need to get started at that office fairly quickly. The sooner the better. We already have a client who wants to meet next week."

Maggie heard what she said, but the offer didn't seem to matter given the current circumstances. What mattered was that Scout had run off crying. There was no telling where she'd gone or how upset she might be.

"I'll call you tomorrow with my answer. Right now

I have to find Scout." Maggie was already heading for the front door as she spoke.

Maggie turned back to Allison once she was there. "Thank you so much for the generous offer. It's an incredible opportunity."

"Yes, it is," Allison said with total confidence. "I hope you take that into consideration when you're thinking about accepting."

She and Maggie stepped into the sunlight, Maggie in a man's T-shirt and two-day worn jeans, and Allison in her designer black business suit and heels.

They shook hands, then Allison turned toward her gray E-Class Mercedes, stepping gently so her heels wouldn't sink into the soft earth.

That's when Maggie once again became acutely aware of her own footwear: cowboy boots, scuffed and caked with mud.

BLAKE HAD JUST gotten into his truck and fired up the ignition when he noticed Scout in his rearview mirror tearing up the road behind him with Suzie by her side.

"What the heck?"

He cut the engine, popped open the door and jumped out, just as his daughter came running into his arms, sobbing. "Oh, Daddy."

Blake picked her up, leaned on the cab of his truck, stroked her back and waited until she pulled herself together. When she could breathe again, he said, "What's wrong, sweetpea? Did you hurt yourself? Are you okay?"

He could feel her little head bob up and down. "So, you're okay?"

"Yes," she whispered.

"You want to tell me what's wrong?"

She slowly shook her head.

"Okay. I was just on my way to town. Want to come with me?"

She nodded and said, "Can Suzie come?"

"She sure can. Anything you want."

Twenty minutes later he was paying for three doughnuts with extra sprinkles, a large coffee with heavy cream, and a hot chocolate with extra marshmallows at Holey Rollers.

"Rough morning, Doc?" Amanda asked from behind the counter as she gave him his change.

"Nothing I can't handle," he told her as he shoved the change in his pocket. He was not about to share his personal life with a teenager.

"So, like, I heard Allison Bennett was up at your place looking for Maggie. Wow, that's like the best thing ever. Allison Bennett is my all-time idol. Is she Maggie's friend or what, Doc?"

"Maggie's never met her before." He walked to his table but Amanda was not about to leave him alone. She grabbed the doughnut plates and followed close behind.

"Then what did she want? She came in here for a coffee and I about died right there behind the bear claws. She ordered a skinny-latte with soy. No wonder. Did you get a look at her? She can't weigh more than a hundred pounds soaking wet. I bet she eats nothing but health food, and jogs every day for about two hours. No doughnuts for her and…"

Amanda wouldn't stop talking, even after she put the plates on the table. "What I wouldn't give to work for someone like Allison Bennett."

Scout's face lit up. "You can take Maggie's job. Then

she won't have to leave Briggs and move to L.A. I don't like L.A. But you might."

"Maggie got a job offer from Allison Bennett?"

Scout took a big bite out of her doughnut as she swung her feet under the table. She nodded up at Amanda as she chewed.

"That is, like, so cool! Oh, wait a minute." She turned to him. "Not cool, right?"

"Amanda, I—"

"That's why you two are in here eating doughnuts. Oh, Doc, I'm, like, so sorry. I didn't even think about you and Maggie and—can I get you anything else, Doc? A jelly doughnut with sprinkles, maybe? Or how about a bear claw? On the house."

"Thanks. I'm fine. It's a great opportunity for Maggie, and I wish her all the best."

Amanda backed away. "Sure, Doc. All the best."

The thing was, Blake had listened to pretty much everything that Allison Bennett had offered Maggie as he stood on the other side of the doorway between the kitchen and hallway. He'd left to get cleaned up right when they were getting into the details of the offer. He didn't want to listen anymore. Had he known Scout was going to react that way, he would never have allowed her to be in the same room.

As it was now, he realized he hadn't been a good father. He'd thought of his own desires instead of how Maggie's going, especially to L.A., would affect his daughter.

He was over that. He had to think of Scout first. Last night would have to be shoved aside. The way he figured it, Maggie hadn't really meant it when she'd answered "me, too" to his blabbing that he loved her. It was her temperature rising that forced her into agreeing with something she had no use for.

Who was he kidding? He could no more keep Maggie from the city than he could teach a bird to jog. And from the look on Maggie's face when she talked about Allison Bennett, he'd probably have better luck with the bird.

He was just about to take a big mouthful of his doughnut when Scout said, "Daddy, I promise when I grow up I won't ever move to L.A."

Blake put the doughnut back down on the plate. "Oh, Scout, is that what this is all about?"

She nodded. "You loved Mommy until she moved to L.A. And you love Maggie and that mean lady wants her to move to L.A. And you love me. But if I move to L.A. you won't love me anymore, too, just like Mommy and Maggie. So, I'm not ever moving to L.A. Maybe California 'cause that's where Disneyland is, but never L.A."

She took a huge bite of her doughnut and multicolored sprinkles stuck to her lips, rolled down her chin, and got caught in her curly hair.

Blake's heart broke wide open. He went over to her and squatted next to her chair to look into her sweet blue eyes. "Scout, I want you to listen to me, okay?"

She nodded, looking all serious even though candy sprinkles were stuck to her little cheeks.

"I could never, ever stop loving you no matter where you live or where you go or what you do. I'm your daddy, and I'll always be your daddy. I didn't stop loving your mommy just because she lives away from us. Part of me will always love your mommy because she gave me you. Your mommy and me just couldn't live together anymore, that's all. But it had nothing to do with her wanting to live in L.A. It had a lot to do with me wanting to live right here with Dodge and Colt and Travis and the boys. Do you understand?"

She thought for a while, then she said, "But what about Maggie? You love Maggie, don't you?" Her eyes welled up again.

He took a deep breath and let it out. He had to be honest with his daughter. "Yes, Scout, I do."

"I love her, too, Daddy, and I don't want her to go away. Can't you stop her, Daddy?"

Great big tears rolled down her cheeks and stuck to the sprinkles. Blake picked her up and carried her outside. He caught Amanda and just about everyone else in the bakery watching him. He was sure they all heard what he'd told Scout.

When they were outside in the crisp September weather he knelt down and stood her in front of him, gently moving the snarl of curls off her face and brushing off the sprinkles. She studied him with such a sad little face that he wanted to cry, as well.

"Baby, I can't keep Maggie here if she doesn't want to stay. None of us can. It's going to be hard for all of us to let her go, but living in the country isn't what she wants for her life. She likes living in the city, it's easier for her. She enjoys going to her job every day, running things and making decisions. People depend on Maggie, and she gets to wear all her nice clothes and high heels, and we have to respect that even if it means we have to watch her go."

"But I don't want her to go, Daddy."

"We can't always have what we want, sweetpea. You know that. And that's why we have to make it easy for

Maggie to decide. You and me. Because we love Maggie, we have to pretend like it's okay for her to leave. That she doesn't have to worry about us, because we'll be fine without her. The job will make Maggie happy, Scout. And you want her to be happy, don't you?"

She nodded, and wiped a tear away with the back of her hand.

"Can you help me to make it easy for Maggie? Allison Bennett has offered Maggie an important job and I know she wants to take it, but she's conflicted because of us."

"What does confl...*conflicted* mean?"

"She doesn't know what she should do."

"She should stay."

He tilted his head and gave her a look, hoping she would finally get it. She said, "Maggie should go with the mean lady so she can be happy."

"That's my girl." He gave her a tight hug.

"Can we go back and finish our doughnuts now? Our drinks are getting cold and I don't like cold hot chocolate. It tastes funny."

Blake stood and took her hand as she skipped her way toward Holey Rollers. He wished he could get over this as quickly as Scout seemed to, but he knew losing Maggie wasn't going to be that easy.

Chapter Fifteen

"I can't find her anywhere," Maggie told Dodge while they stood in front of the beautiful chestnut-colored horse Maggie had seen Colt riding the previous morning. Dodge had spent the past half hour brushing the horse while she frantically searched for Scout.

"She's around. Don't go gettin' all worked up," he told her. "That child never strays too far. Suzie won't let her."

"Dodge, I've looked everywhere, even under the beds, and I can't find her or the dog. Shouldn't we call the police or something? You don't understand. She ran out of the house crying. She hates me or she hates Allison. I couldn't really tell. But that doesn't matter. How can you just keep brushing that horse? It's been more than an hour. We need to do something."

Maggie stomped her foot and the horse whinnied. Dodge stopped brushing and turned to Maggie. "You're gonna cause sweet Jezebel, here, to get all riled up. Calm down, Maggie. There ain't no cause to be worryin' none before we know all the facts."

Dodge ushered Maggie out of the stall, then closed the gate behind them.

"Time is of the essence with a missing child."

Dodge chuckled. "She ain't missin', she just ain't been found yet."

"I can't handle this. I'm going to call the police."

"Don't have no police in Briggs. Only got a sheriff and he's down in the next county. Take him near an hour to drive all the way up here, and by then I suspect Scout'll turn up. He won't like ruinin' his day over somethin' that ain't real."

"Dodge, listen to me. Scout is missing."

He pushed his hat back on his head. "It seems to me like there's two kinds of missin'. One is when you put something somewhere and you can't remember where that somewhere is, or you think something or someone should be where you think they should be, but they're really somewhere's else. Which is it?"

Maggie was baffled by his logic. "The second one, I guess."

"Don't you know?"

She wanted to scream. Her voice moved up an octave. "Okay. She's not missing, she's gone."

"That makes more sense. Gone where?"

"I—I can't do this anymore. I'm going in the house and calling the sheriff."

"Okay, but isn't that Blake drivin' on up toward the house?" He pointed behind her.

Maggie swung around and sure enough, Blake's truck was pulling up to the front of the house. She watched as he parked and two seconds later Maggie could see two little feet clad in pink cowboy boots hit the blacktop. Her heart leaped up to her throat. She was never so happy to see someone in her entire life. Emotion overtook her as she ran toward Scout, Suzy and Blake.

When she came up close, she swooped Scout up in her arms and gave her a tight hug. "I didn't know where you were. I'm so glad you're okay."

"Of course I'm okay. Daddy took me to Holey Rollers and we ate a bunch of doughnuts with sprinkles. We brought some home. You want one?" She held up a white bag.

"No. Thanks," Maggie told her and put her back down on the ground. Scout instantly ran over to Dodge, yelling about bringing home doughnuts while waving the bag in the air. Suzie and Mush joined in the ruckus and greeted each other with barks and sniffs.

Maggie stood stock-still, staring at Blake. A mixture of anger and relief pulsed through her veins.

Blake said, "Sorry if you were worried. I didn't know you were looking for—"

But Maggie couldn't hold it in any longer. She lashed out. "I looked everywhere for her. I thought something horrible happened. I can't believe you took her and didn't tell anyone. How could you do that?"

He stepped toward her. "First off, you need to take a deep breath and relax."

"I can't relax. That was the most important moment of my life and I couldn't even enjoy it or finish talking to Allison Bennett because Scout decided to throw some sort of fit and run out of the house. Do you even know how embarrassing that was for me? Not to mention that I couldn't find her and Dodge kept talking in circles. And you had her the entire time. Would it have killed you to call me?"

Blake's face went all serious. "Your phone is dead, remember? And since when do I have to check in with you when I take my own daughter for a drive?"

"That's not the point and you know it."

"Then what is the point, Maggie? Because a month from now when you're sitting in your shiny new office in L.A., both Scout and me will be a mere memory and it won't matter one lick where she is or what she's doing. This whole thing—Scout, me, Kitty, all of us—we were temporary until you got what you wanted. Well, you've got it, so why don't you save all of us more grief and just go. We were getting along fine before you showed up and we'll get along fine after you've left."

Hot tears stung Maggie's eyes as she watched him walk past her and head for the house. "Blake, wait, I—"

But he just kept walking.

FOR THE NEXT FEW days, Maggie tried to immerse herself in the wonders of her new job. She called the recruiter at Technix and told them thank you, but no thank you. Then she phoned Allison and accepted the position at her company. Allison couldn't have been nicer and immediately set Maggie up with someone to help with the move, which would be happening the very next Sunday.

She'd tried to get some comfort out of Amanda or Cori but neither woman would cooperate. Amanda avoided waiting on her at Holey Rollers, and Cori gave her the cold shoulder when she stopped by Kitty's house to visit the twins.

That was when it hit her that she was actually going to leave Briggs and move to Los Angeles. When she cried for twenty-four hours straight she knew something wasn't quite right, but by then it was too late to do anything about it. The horse was out of the barn. The die had been cast. The pickle had been brined.

Or, Maggie's new-found favorite, the bull had sniffed the heifer.

"As long as you're still breathing there are always options," Kitty told her as they sat together in the nursery, each holding a baby, trying to get the last little burps out of them while rocking in dual swivel rockers. The rocking chairs were big and plush and Maggie had decided the first piece of furniture she would buy for her apartment in Brentwood would be one of these rockers. They were like heaven.

"Not this time," Maggie countered. "The position with Allison is everything I've worked for. Everything I've ever dreamed of. It's perfect. And besides, I've already accepted the offer. I can't back down now."

Mrs. Abernathy came in and placed a tray with tea, finger sandwiches and cookies on the dresser. "I thought you might be getting hungry, Kitty. Gotta eat or you won't make enough milk for them babies." And she turned and left, completely ignoring Maggie.

"She hates me," Maggie said.

"No, she doesn't. You know that's just her way."

"There's only one cup on the tray," Maggie said as emotion overtook her...again.

"Okay, she's a bit miffed. But so am I. If this job is so wonderful, why can't you stop crying?"

Tears streamed down Maggie's face. She cried more than the babies did. "I don't know," she said as she tried to get her emotions under control.

Jessica and Parker let out simultaneous burps, causing Maggie to laugh out loud. "So much for my tears," she told Kitty as she moved Parker off her shoulder and rested him on her lap, his watchful eyes staring up at her.

"You're a natural, Maggie. Look how content he is."

"Don't or I'm going to start crying again."

Kitty rocked faster in her chair. "Fine, but tell me one thing, and be honest because I can always tell if you're lying. Are you in love with Doc Blake?"

Maggie didn't want to answer. She didn't want to admit the truth even to herself much less her sister. Besides, what did it matter now? She was leaving.

"He hates me."

"Where did you ever get that idea?"

"You weren't there. You didn't see his face when he told me to leave."

"Guys do that to protect themselves, especially guys like Blake. He's a dad, and you see the way Tim protects these babies. He'd do anything to keep them safe and happy."

"So you think he said all that because he was protecting Scout?" Her voice caught in her throat.

"I've been wanting to tell you this for days, but you've been too upset. Amanda told Milo, who told Mrs. Abernathy, who told Cori, who told Tim, who told me that she was behind the counter at Holey Rollers that day you thought something happened to Scout, and she said Scout was crying because you were moving to L.A. You've got to understand, sweetie, that Scout's mom lives in L.A. Bethany stayed there when Doc and Scout moved to Briggs, and Scout hasn't seen her since. To Scout, L.A. might as well be some black hole where everyone who goes there never returns."

Maggie dried her eyes on the cloth diaper she had draped over her shoulder to catch Parker's spit-up. "I knew Bethany lived in Los Angeles, but I… Why didn't somebody tell me this before? So that's why Scout went crazy on Allison, and that's why she ran out of the house. I had no idea."

"The benefits of a small town."

"But I said some horrible things to Blake about how Scout ruined my meeting with Allison. I really didn't mean to say that. I don't know what came over me. I was so frantic to find Scout. Then when she showed up with Blake offering me a doughnut, like everything was fine, when it clearly was not, I guess I lost it."

"You both did. But you still haven't answered my question. Are you in love with him?"

This time Maggie didn't hesitate. "More than anything."

Blake decided he could get along fine without Maggie in the office for a few weeks, until Kitty could return. He'd hired Amanda part-time. She'd started dating one of Tim's many cousins, so she didn't seem to be interested in Doc anymore, a situation he welcomed.

"Besides," she told him on her first day, "until you, like, resolve this thing with Maggie, you won't be a good catch for anybody."

"Thanks," he told her.

"Anytime," she said, straight-faced.

She had a point. Getting along without Maggie in the office was easy, but getting along without Maggie in his bed wasn't working out, as well. For five nights running he hadn't been able to sleep more than a few hours. This was something new for Blake. He could always sleep no matter what the upheaval in his life; not even when Scout was a baby did he have trouble falling back to sleep. And not even when he'd drink a gallon of coffee trying to stay awake to study for finals in college. Nothing kept Blake Granger from getting his eight.

Nothing, until he walked away from Maggie Daniels.

Replacing her in his life was proving to be impossible. He tried to act as if she didn't matter; however, it was like trying to scratch your ear with your elbow. It wasn't going to happen. At least not anytime soon.

"You know she leaves on Sunday," Liza, his dental assistant, relayed to him as he filled a molar for one of his older patients, Milo's brother, Jethro. Both he and Liza wore light blue masks over their noses and mouths, so their speech was a bit muffled.

Jethro calmed himself by listening to his music on his tiny Nano, and fortunately couldn't hear a word they said.

"Suction. Yes, you've already told me, several times."

Liza vacuumed saliva and a tiny chunk of composite from Jethro's mouth.

"I just wanted to make sure you heard me."

Blake finished packing the tooth.

"How could I not? You've been reminding me every hour for the past week. Water."

Liza sprayed the new filling, then sucked out the excess water, drying it with air.

"You can stop her if you want to."

"I tried that once before with my ex. It doesn't work. Light."

"Maggie's different."

He held the spectrometer, a blue LED light, on the filling waiting for it to set and harden.

"Cut from the same cloth."

"The design might be the same, but this fabric's pure silk."

"Silk's expensive. I don't have that kind of money. Never will."

"Maggie's capable of spinning her own silk."

"Not in Briggs she's not. This town's not made for silk. We're more into potato sacks."

He handed the spectrometer back to Liza. She handed him the small blue articulating paper.

"She's a clever girl. Don't sell her short."

He placed the blue paper in Jethro's mouth above the new filling while still holding on to it with tweezers.

"Bite down," he told Jethro in a loud voice. Jethro obliged. "I'm not selling her. She sold me, and the sale was final."

No excess blue on Jethro's upper teeth. The filling was perfect. Blake pulled his mask down below his chin and tapped his patient's shoulder to get his attention. "All finished, Jethro. You were great."

Jethro beamed as the chair automatically moved upright. He pulled his earphones out of his ears and said, "No sale is ever final, Doc. You can always change your mind."

Blake looked at him. "I thought you couldn't hear us with that music blasting in your ears."

"One of the buds is dead. I dropped it in the toilet while I was going."

Blake didn't respond. The visual was too disgusting.

SATURDAY NIGHT HAD finally arrived, and Maggie was all ready to leave the next morning. The tears had stopped flowing and she had made up her mind that leaving Briggs was the best thing for all concerned.

Now, as she sat alone in the living room, on the scratchy sofa, channel surfing at eight-twenty-three at night while everyone else in the house was trying to get some sleep, she couldn't stop thinking about those delicious rare steaks over at Belly Up.

Kitty had made a delightful dinner of roasted beets and garbanzo beans with a side of cranberry couscous. Tim had devoured it readily, but Maggie had only picked at it and now her stomach was growling for real food.

She hadn't actually left the house for more than an hour or so over the past week, not wanting to run into anyone she knew and have to deal with their wrath or be away too long from Kitty and the babies. It only made her cry harder. But she felt stronger tonight, strong enough to handle everyone's loyalty to Doctor Blake Granger.

And besides, how could she possibly leave Briggs without one more Idaho steak and a real Idaho baked potato?

She absolutely had to have it now.

Maggie clicked off the TV, quietly ran up the hallway for her coat and scarf, and slipped on the ratty pair of boots Kitty had given her as a reminder of Briggs. Within minutes she was out the front door on her way to Belly Up.

It was cold outside, cold with snow flurries. Normally, Maggie hated cold weather. She was the warm-weather type, more suited to Los Angeles than even the Bay Area, where it could get down into the thirties in winter. And in Briggs it would certainly get below zero and stay there for weeks. How could she possibly even think of staying?

She told herself she would never be able to handle it. Still, as the snow fell faster and the flakes grew bigger, she felt as if she were stuck in a magical snow globe. It was positively beautiful and amazingly quiet. A few ornate street lights illuminated the sidewalk, giving off a golden glow and making her surroundings look surreal. No cars. No other people. Just snow settling in on a small town. She fastened her red scarf tighter around her neck and burrowed into her warm coat, slipping her gloved hands into her pockets. If she were in Brentwood right now she would probably be wearing a tank top and flip-flops.

Somehow, she liked this much better. Go figure.

She gazed up at the gray sky and watched as thousands of big snowflakes came tumbling down on her. The visual caused her to stop walking, open her mouth and catch a snowflake on her tongue, then another and another until she laughed out loud as they tickled her face and lips. She let go and twirled for a moment, opening her arms as if she wanted to capture the evening and give it a farewell hug. As she spun, she could feel herself getting dizzy. A sensation she hadn't felt since she was a kid. It made her giggle.

"You know you won't be able to do this in L.A.," Blake said. She stopped twirling and stared at him. "I think the last time it snowed there, Teddy Roosevelt was in office."

He was incredibly handsome in a black overcoat, black jeans and boots with a sky-blue scarf wrapped around his neck. His face glistened with a rosy glow from the cold.

She wanted to fall into his arms. She wanted him to beg her to stay, tell her again that he loved her. She wanted to hear the words tumble from his beautiful mouth, so she could tell him how much she loved him in return.

But he didn't.

"Harry S. Truman. Although it did hail enough in February of twenty-eleven that it appeared to be snow."

"I was just guessing."

"I'm not."

"How do you know these things?"

"I had to look it up for a client once."

His eyes sparkled under the street lights. He wasn't wearing a hat, so the snow caught in his hair. She thought about how handsome he would look when his hair turned gray, and how much she'd like to see that.

"You like that kind of thing, don't you?"

"What kind of thing?" She'd been lost in her dreams of him in the future.

"Knowing trivia."

"Yes, but only when it has some relevance."

"What's the relevance in knowing when the last snowfall was in L.A.?"

"So I know how to pack. I'm moving there tomorrow."

The words seemed to strike him and he grimaced for a split second.

Now, she thought. *Kiss me now, and tell me not to leave.*

He gazed down at the sidewalk then back at her. "Yes, I know. Are you excited?" He threw her a tepid smile.

"It's everything I've worked for."

He nodded, then after a beat he said, "Where are you headed?"

"Thought I'd grab a steak before I left. Where are you headed?"

"To apologize to a friend."

His words caught her off guard. Her throat tightened and her eyes watered a little, but she pushed the tears away.

"I'd like to do the same."

"Seems as if we've just accomplished that mission."

"Easier than I thought it would be," she said, searching his eyes, yearning for a sign so she could go to him.

But there was none.

"For me, too."

"Well, then." She suddenly felt awkward and strange. As if they hardly knew each other. Neither one said a word as the minutes slipped by, as they stood there, silent, under the streetlight. Maggie was desperate to see him smile again, hoping more than anything he would ask her to stay.

But as soon as she thought it, she knew she couldn't. She knew she had to go. She would never be able to live with herself if she walked away from this job offer. It was perfect for her, everything she ever wanted, and as tough as this was she knew she had no choice but to leave.

A car whizzed by, startling her. The sound of its tires on the snowy ground were like sandpaper on her nerves. It broke the silence between them with a jolt of reality. She wasn't standing in a snow globe with her lover. She was standing on the sidewalk in Briggs, Idaho, with her ex-lover.

The thought tore at her heart.

"You know, people will talk if we're seen together."

He gave her that adorable grin of his and suddenly she felt all warm and hopeful inside.

"It's expected. It's a small town."

"Will it bother you?"

"A little, but I can handle it."

He was taking a step closer, like he was going to kiss her, when her phone vibrated in her pocket. She tried to ignore it, but on this quiet street even Blake could hear it. "You better take that," he said, moving back. "It might be important."

She pulled the phone out of her pocket. It was Allison calling her for the umpteenth time. She hadn't even officially started her job yet and the woman must have called her fifteen times in the past two days alone. There was always something she needed Maggie to handle with the business or with a potential client.

"It's Allison," Maggie explained. She hesitated, not wanting to take the call, but she knew Allison would keep calling until she answered.

"Go ahead. I understand."

"Blake, I—"

"It's getting late, anyway. I'd best be heading on home. This snow looks as if it's going to keep coming down and the road to the ranch can be tough to get down."

Her phone stopped buzzing, and a moment later started up again. She cleared the tension that was forming in her throat. "I better answer this."

She started to pull a hand out of her pocket wanting to touch him one last time, but she knew if she did, she wouldn't ever stop.

"Maggie, I…" He looked down, then back at Maggie. "I wish you nothing but the best, no matter where you go or what you do."

She couldn't stop the tear that slipped down her cheek. "Thanks. You, too."

Maggie didn't want to do this anymore, didn't want to deal with the bundle of emotions welling up inside her so she gave him a brief smile and turned away from him to answer her phone.

"Hi, Allison."

"Did I catch you at a bad time?"

Maggie heard Blake get into his truck. It took every ounce of willpower she had to keep her feet planted on that snowy sidewalk.

"No. Not at all," she lied. "Your timing's perfect."

As Blake drove away, he threw her a smile and a wave. She waved back, completely heartbroken, but confident she had made the right decision. Meanwhile, Allison went on about the multimillion-dollar media blitz she would be handling for Aragon Computers.

Chapter Sixteen

As Blake drove away, he felt about as melancholy as a hound dog sitting on the porch of a deserted cabin. He had desperately wanted to rock her in his arms and plead with her not to go, but that phone call had come before he could have made a fool out of himself.

The thing that stuck in his craw was how easily he had allowed himself to think she might be different when all the signs were there. It couldn't have been more spelled out for him if she had told him point-blank: *Blake Granger, I'm going to tease and torment you, then I'm going to make love to you until your very bones call out for mercy, act as if I love you, then kick the crap out of your heart and leave you in the dust.*

He shook his head at the thought of her on the phone, walking back to Kitty's. Apparently, that steak wasn't important anymore.

Part of him had wanted to beg her to stay, but he knew she couldn't and wouldn't, no matter what he did or said. Instead, he had shoved his love for her aside and driven off, hoping he could make her disappear as easily as he'd waved goodbye.

Funny thing was, the more he thought about her

telling him exactly what would happen, the more he knew he wouldn't have changed a thing.

How could he? He had fallen in love with her as soon as he'd seen that beautiful face of hers, looking all full of herself and entirely kissable.

The snow was coming down heavier as Blake drove home. It stuck to his windshield, making it difficult to see. He wasn't in the mood to fight the weather. Still, he didn't want to go home. He didn't want to be reminded of Maggie when he passed that empty guest room or when he slept in his empty bed. He needed to talk to somebody. He needed somebody who would understand.

He needed to talk to his brother Colt.

"COME ON IN, big brother. I had a feeling you'd be showing up here tonight. I just put the boys down, so we're free until one of them wakes up calling for something."

Blake followed Colt into his living room. A fire burned in the hearth as Colt picked up trucks, game pieces and his boys' clothes off the floor. "Can I get you something? You look as though you might be in need of a bit of liquid warmth."

"Brandy. Thanks," Blake told him, knowing that what he really needed was some advice, but was too self-conscious to ask for it.

By the time Colt returned with two glasses of brandy, Blake had stoked the fire, removed his coat and gloves, and settled on one end of the brown sofa. Colt's house was decorated in contemporary masculine functional. All the feminine pieces his wife had bought were stored out in the barn or had been given away.

"So what's up, big brother?" Colt asked, handing him a glass of amber liquid.

"You know exactly what's up."

Colt took a sip of his brandy. "I thought I'd be polite and let you tell me."

"Since when have you become polite?"

"Since I know losing Maggie is ripping out your insides."

Blake stared down at his drink. "Mind if I stay here tonight?"

"Already set up the spare room."

"You're a good brother, Colt."

"I learned from the best," he said then slammed his brandy back in one gulp and stood. "You want to talk, I'll listen. If not, I'm heading off to bed. Them boys of mine start an early day."

Blake changed his mind about needing to talk. It was enough that his brother understood what he was going through. "You go on to bed. I'll sit here for a while. Get my bearings. Thanks for the brandy."

"Anytime, big brother."

Blake stood and the two men hugged. Colt went off to bed, dragging with him as many toys and clothes as he could hold. Blake switched off the lights and sat staring at the roaring fire, trying to sort out how he was going to learn to live without Maggie Daniels in his life.

MAGGIE'S NEW JOB turned out to be everything she ever wanted in terms of a career. Not only was she back on track in a spacious corner office, but she had out-done even her wildest dreams. Sure, she hardly saw her posh apartment on Gorham Avenue in Brentwood, and she rarely enjoyed a night out on trendy San Vincente Boulevard, but she had personally landed four new major clients in the few weeks since she'd been in Los Angeles. And Allison seemed duly impressed with her performance.

Maggie was finally living her dream: designer clothes, a fancy new car, hobnobbing with the rich and famous, and a plush sofa made of the finest synthetic fiber her money could buy. She even sprang for a rocker exactly like Kitty's.

So, why with all that she had going for her was she more miserable than ever?

She hated all the traffic in L.A., the bad air caused her throat to feel scratchy most of the time, and the tile floor in her ultramodern apartment made her feet chronically cold. Then there were the endless paved roads and the complete anonymity that she once enjoyed, but now hated. And she couldn't get over how expensive everything seemed. Had the prices doubled or was she simply mentally caught up in the Briggs economy?

Strange as it seemed, she longed for a wide-open sky, especially at night when all the stars were hidden from view by the lights of the city. She missed the smell of pine, and the feel of snowflakes on her tongue.

She didn't exactly understand what was happening to her, but she was finding it more and more difficult to remain focused.

Big-city diva Maggie Daniels was desperately homesick for small-town Briggs and there was absolutely nothing she could do about it. She had made her bed and now she was struggling with the covers.

At first, she thought she simply needed a period of

adjustment. The city was something she had to grow back into, like getting used to riding a bike again after you'd given it up for a long stretch of time. Unfortunately, it was more than a simple feeling of being unsteady; she honestly didn't want to ride anymore.

"Now what?" she asked herself as she gazed into the bathroom mirror.

It was the day before Thanksgiving and Maggie was preparing to fly business class to London, England, in less than four hours. It was the biggest deal of her life. If she landed this client, which seemed inevitable, she would secure her standing with her new company and prove to herself that she and Allison Bennett were indeed at the top of their game.

As she dressed for the long flight—jeans, a simple cream-colored sweater and fuzzy warm socks under knee-high black boots—she tried to stay positive. After all, she was on her way to London. How great was that? Allison's company was doing so well they had to hire more people in both offices.

Maggie Daniels had, indeed, arrived.

The only fly in her London pie was Kitty's insistence that she return to Briggs for Thanksgiving. More than anything, Maggie would love to return to Briggs, but she knew she couldn't. For one thing, she couldn't possibly postpone the meeting in London, and for another, she couldn't pour salt on the Blake wound. Not now, anyway. For the most part, she had her feelings for him in check, and she wanted to keep them that way for the foreseeable future. It was her only hope of survival in this cement-and-metal jungle. Besides, she hadn't spent the holidays with Kitty since they were girls.

And just as she was about to pull on those black

boots, feeling confident in her holiday convictions, her phone rang. Naturally, it was Kitty. Her sister seemed to have a sort of radar. Whenever Maggie thought about her, she called.

Or it could be that she'd been calling every day at the same time for the past week trying to convince Maggie to come home for Thanksgiving. Not that Kitty's house was "home," but it was the closest thing to home that Maggie had felt in a very long time.

"What's up, sis?" Maggie chirped into the phone, as if she had no idea why Kitty was calling so early in the morning. She abandoned her boots in favor of gathering up more of her things to toss into the open suitcase.

"You know what's up. Tomorrow's Thanksgiving. Everybody wants to see you. Tell me you've booked a flight and you'll be here in time for dinner tomorrow night," Kitty said. Maggie could hear the apprehension in her voice. "My babies miss their auntie."

"Your babies are too young to know they even have an auntie."

"They'd know their auntie if she were around more."

"That's not possible."

"Anything is possible. You just have to decide to make it happen."

"I don't have time for this."

"What do you have time for?"

Maggie pulled her winter coat off a hanger in the closet, but it slipped out of her hands and landed on Kitty's cowboy boots.

Her breath caught in her throat. She blew it out. "My flight to London leaves in a few hours and I'm not ready."

"Only people without families go to London on

Thanksgiving. You have a family and we want you here."

Maggie stood, picking up her coat then closing the door on the closet, trying to ignore those scuffed-up boots that she'd grown to love. Maggie had gotten good at not letting Kitty get to her, telling herself to be strong. To focus on her goals. To be a big girl. "I'm not going to be able to make it this year, but I promise to fly in for Christmas."

Kitty let out a long sigh. "You're doing it again, you know."

"Doing what?" But Maggie knew exactly what she was referring to.

"Putting your job before your family."

Maggie paused, trying to get her nerves to settle down. Her morning coffee had turned to acid in her stomach. "You don't understand. I don't have a choice."

"That's the old Maggie talking. The new Maggie knows she always has a choice."

"Not today. Not this week."

She tossed her coat on top of her suitcase, walked back to the closet, opened the door, grabbed the cowboy boots and proceeded to slip them on, thinking they might keep her feet warmer than the thin, expensive boots she'd been going to wear. Then she shoved the expensive boots in her suitcase, just in case cowboy boots looked a little out there in London.

"It's a national holiday about giving thanks. Isn't it time you celebrated it with your family?"

An intense feeling of nausea swept over Maggie. She didn't want to talk to Kitty anymore. "I can't do this now. I have to finish packing."

"Are you giving me the brush-off?"

She hated it when Kitty could peg her so easily. "Of course not. You're my sister. I'm just in a hurry."

"And instead you're talking to your pest of a sister, is that it?"

Maggie could hear one of the babies fussing in the background. Her eyes watered as emotion gripped her. She'd give almost anything to hold those sweet babies again. "No, that's not it at all. Please, don't do this. You know how important working for Allison is to me."

"Apparently, more important than I am, or your niece and nephew, who change every day and you're missing everything."

Maggie couldn't talk to Kitty anymore or she'd start blubbering like a kid. If she gave Kitty any inkling that she was miserable, Kitty would be all over her like a flea in a doghouse.

The thought reminded her of Blake, but as soon as she thought of him she dismissed the image and concentrated on the task at hand…to appease Kitty.

"I'll be there at Christmas. How much can they change by Christmas?" Maggie knew she was lying, but she had no choice. She was desperate.

"And when Christmas rolls around, what excuse will you give me then?"

Maggie sighed. Who was she trying to fool? Certainly not Kitty. She'd already played this corporate game and lost. "Lately, I can't talk to you without it turning into an argument."

"Why is pointing out the truth an argument?"

Maggie had another incoming call. It was the limo driver, probably calling to tell her he was out front waiting for her. "I really have to go. My driver's here."

"Fine, but I hope this job is enough for you, because it's all you're ever going to have."

"Kitty, you don't understand, I... Kitty, are you still there?"

Silence, then the familiar sound indicating that the caller had hung up.

Maggie returned the driver's call. She told him she'd be out in ten minutes and proceeded to cry like a baby while staring down at her now warm feet tucked inside Kitty's cowboy boots.

It was at that exact moment when everything finally came into focus. When she realized her chronically cold feet were suddenly warm, and what Blake had really meant when he'd scolded her outside his office door on that first day when she was too scared to go inside. She had learned something about herself that day, something she'd truly never believed she possessed, and needed now more than she'd ever needed anything in her entire life.

A backbone.

THREE DAYS AGO, Dodge had alerted the Granger family that they might have to stop by Kitty's at some point on Thanksgiving. And yesterday during breakfast, Dodge warned Blake that Kitty was getting pretty determined about them not only stopping by, but sharing the main course. Then on Thanksgiving morning, before Dodge could get the thirty-pound bird into the oven, Kitty phoned to invite the entire Granger clan for a sit-down dinner at six o'clock that night.

"I'd be so disappointed if any of you couldn't make it," she had told Doc before he could reason away the invitation. He'd wanted to use the bad weather excuse—it had snowed more than two feet the previous night—but Kitty knew the Grangers had their very own snowplow.

"We'll do our best, Kitty" was about all Blake could say before he hung up.

Dodge, who happened to be standing not two feet away, preparing the turkey, simply covered the large roasting pan with a lid and slipped it back into the fridge. "We'll just save this here bird for tomorrow's dinner. I'll call your brothers and tell them the news. They'll react better if it comes from me."

Blake admitted he was somewhat skeptical—okay completely skeptical—about celebrating Thanksgiving at Kitty's house, but the woman simply would not take no for an answer. So the entire Granger clan had little choice but to suck it up and accept the invitation.

The kids were warned to be polite and not to comment negatively on whatever bean-nut-tofu concoction Kitty put down in front of them, but Blake wasn't so sure they could control their facial expressions, especially Scout.

"I know we've been over this a hundred times, but please try to pretend you like Kitty's dinner," he warned as he pulled up in front of Kitty's place and parked curbside. Through Kitty's front windows, he could see that Colt and his boys had already arrived. Cars and trucks and SUVs crowded the driveway and the surrounding street. Blake figured Kitty must have invited half the town to this tofu feast.

Misery loved company.

"Are you going to pretend?" Scout asked with that soft innocent voice of hers. He shut off the ignition and turned to her behind him. "Yes. To be polite, I'm going to pretend I love everything on my dinner plate."

"But isn't that lying, Daddy? You don't like tofu turkey roll."

Dodge, who was sitting in the passenger seat, also turned to her. "Lying to somebody when you're tryin' to protect your rotten ways is like makin' a pact with the devil. One day it'll catch up and bite you on your cute bottom. But when you pretend for no other reason than you're wantin' to make somebody happy, then you're makin' a pact with an angel and nothin' but good will come to you."

She considered this for several seconds. "So, then, Kitty will be happy if I tell her I like tofu when I really don't?"

"Yes," Dodge replied.

"But then, what if she gives me more tofu and I have to pretend again and then she'll give me even more, and I get sick from eating all that yucky tofu. What do I do if I want to throw up?"

Blake chuckled as he slipped from the cab, then helped his daughter out of the backseat. "Scout, I want you to go in there and be respectful to Kitty. You don't have to do anything or eat anything you don't want to. All I ask is that you act nice. Will you at least do that?"

"Oh, Daddy, why didn't you just tell me that a long time ago? That's easy."

And she raced to the front door full of smiles. When she got there, someone opened it and she raced inside.

"That one is smarter than both of us combined," Dodge said as he carried an extra-large bowl of his mashed spuds. His father could do without almost anything else on Thanksgiving, but he adamantly refused

to try to make it through dinner without mashed potatoes made with real butter and cream, both of which
Kitty feared.

Ever since Maggie had left, Blake didn't care much
about potatoes or turkeys or tofu. Nothing seemed to
matter to him except Scout.

And he certainly would not be proceeding up Kitty's
sidewalk right now if he thought there was any chance
Maggie might be there. Truth was, the only reason he
had agreed to any of this was because Amanda had
told him a couple of days ago she'd heard that Maggie
was on her way to London to score some megadeal.

That suited Blake just fine. The farther away Maggie was the better. It gave him the freedom to live
his daily life without having to think about seeing her
again, because he knew if he did, there was no telling
what kind of fool he might make out of himself.

Dodge made his way ahead of Blake, slipping inside
the house as soon as he arrived at the front door. Blake
lagged behind, suddenly not wanting to be there. Not
wanting to go inside and listen to people talking about
Maggie and how great she was doing with her new job
or how happy she was flying all over the world, perfectly content to be living in a city again.

It wasn't that he didn't want Maggie to be happy. He
simply didn't want to know she could be happy without
him when he was so miserable without her.

"Hi, Doc," Maggie said from the shadows when he
finally stepped up on the porch. He turned and spotted her, bundled up in a blanket, sitting on the swing.

Reason told him to get right back to his truck and
drive away, but emotion made him go closer. "I thought
you were in London on business."

"I decided not to go."

"Didn't your new boss have something to say about that?"

"She didn't like it very much. Threatened to fire me."

He took a couple more steps toward the swing. "How did you convince her otherwise?"

"I didn't. I quit."

He was next to the swing, not truly believing what he had just heard. "Did you say you quit?"

She nodded.

He speculated on the kind of game she was playing. Could it be a play for more money, or a bigger stake in the company? Did she get recruited from an even bigger rival? Why else would she quit something she had worked so hard to achieve? "For another job?" he finally asked.

"In a way, yes."

"Ah, I thought so. I had a feeling you wouldn't give up that kind of action unless you had something else up your sleeve. What is it? Did a bigger company offer you more money?"

"No, nothing like that." She shifted to make room on the swing. "I finally realized my sister is a very smart woman. Much smarter than I'll ever be."

The cold was getting to him as the breeze slipped right through his jacket, so he sat down next to her. She offered to share her blanket. He took her up on the offer and covered his legs. Being that close triggered his body into wanting her, but he kept his distance.

"Thanks. So tell me, how do you figure Kitty's smarter than you?"

"She kept telling me how I always have options, but

I never really considered what she was saying until I thought I had to get on that plane for London. That's when it suddenly hit me. I was going to London to close a deal that *I* personally had put together for a company *I* worked for."

"Sounds like your job description."

"Yes, but I was thinking all wrong and have been for several years now. You taught me that. I can be and do whatever I want—all it takes is warm feet and a backbone."

"You lost me, sweetheart."

"Do you remember what you said to me that day outside of your office when I was afraid of Cori's boys?"

"Probably a lot of nonsense. I might have said just about anything to get you inside."

"You said, and I quote, 'You've got cold feet. It happens, but I know you can do this, and once you find your backbone you're gonna do just fine.'"

He grinned. "Yep. Sounds desperate enough."

"I think I finally found my backbone for good this time. I'm opening my own company. Already started the process, and that client in London? She won't sign with Allison. She wants to work with me, and only me. Go figure."

Blake sat back on the swing and gave it a little push with his foot as he watched the snow accumulate on the porch railing in front of him. He was glad Maggie was opening her own company, glad she'd found the backbone to do it, but all this did was send her right back to L.A., probably as soon as dinner was over.

"I'm happy for you," he said, trying to be polite, but feeling like a complete fraud. He immediately thought of what Scout had told him about getting sick on Kitty's tofu.

"Thanks," Maggie said, standing and heading for the door.

Then, before he could stop himself, Blake shot off the swing and went after her, grabbing her shoulders and spinning her around, still holding on to her. "I love you, Maggie, do you hear me? I love you, and I'm not happy for you. Not happy at all if it means you're going to leave me again. I've tried, but I can't live without you. I want you here, with me, and if that means we have to work something out where you're traveling for part of the time, then so be it. But you're under my skin, Maggie. You're part of who I am now, and I can't lose you again." He gently shook her. "Do you hear me? I want you with me. I want to marry you."

Maggie went all limp and leaned against him, crying. "Me, too. I love you, too."

He kissed her hard, with all the passion and love he could muster. She felt good against his body, like she belonged, and nothing was ever going to change that.

She pulled away, almost giddy with laughter, but he wanted to kiss her and never stop.

"Blake," she said, avoiding his lips. "Blake, listen for a minute. I'm staying right here in Briggs. We don't have to work something out. I've already done that. I'm opening my own company here. I don't need to work for the Allisons of the world. I can do it all myself, with you and Scout by my side. I've come home, Blake, and this time I'm here to stay."

The sound of applause spilled out onto the porch as Blake realized the entire gang had been watching and listening through an open window.

"Can we eat now?" Joey asked once the applause had died down.

"I think that's a mighty fine suggestion," Blake said, as he escorted Maggie into the house.

As soon as they stepped inside, Blake spotted Dodge coming out of the kitchen carrying the biggest golden-brown turkey he had ever seen.

"Is that for real?" he asked Maggie.

"Yep. Kitty made a concession just for you Grangers. Colt flew all the way to Boulder, Colorado, to pick up a turkey from an organic farm. One that Kitty approved of."

"When did this happen?"

"Yesterday, right after I called her to tell her I was coming home."

"Ya gotta love Kitty."

"Smartest woman in the world."

He kissed Maggie again and escorted her into the dining room where a conglomeration of tables were set up for thirty people, which included Cori—who gave Maggie a huge hug—her family, Tim's parents, the Granger clan and Mrs. Abernathy, who said she wouldn't leave those babies for nothin'.

Blake and Maggie took their seats at the end of the table next to Scout, who seemed to be beaming.

"This is the best Thanksgiving ever!" Scout exclaimed at the top of her voice.

"And why is that, Scout?" Blake asked, as everyone else found their seats around the table, with Tim at the head and Kitty right next to him.

The room suddenly went quiet; everyone seemed to be listening to Scout. "Because Maggie came back, and Kitty's babies were born, and Tim came home from the war, and because I love everybody in this room, but mostly because we have a really big turkey."

"No finer prayer of thanks was ever said," Dodge announced as he bowed his head.

"Amen," Blake said, gazing across the table at his sweet little girl who had just managed to say everything everyone was probably thinking.

"Now can we eat?" Joey asked with his fork in the air.

"Now we can eat," Kitty agreed.

Blake reached under the table and took Maggie's hand, knowing that for the rest of his life, this feisty city woman with the most incredible Country heart, had finally come home.

* * * * *

REQUEST YOUR FREE BOOKS!

2 FREE NOVELS PLUS 2 FREE GIFTS!

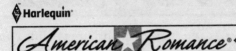

❦ Harlequin®

American ★ Romance®

LOVE, HOME & HAPPINESS

YES! Please send me 2 FREE Harlequin® American Romance® novels and my 2 FREE gifts (gifts are worth about $10). After receiving them, if I don't wish to receive any more books, I can return the shipping statement marked "cancel." If I don't cancel, I will receive 4 brand-new novels every month and be billed just $4.49 per book in the U.S. or $5.24 per book in Canada. That's a saving of at least 14% off the cover price! It's quite a bargain! Shipping and handling is just 50¢ per book in the U.S. and 75¢ per book in Canada.* I understand that accepting the 2 free books and gifts places me under no obligation to buy anything. I can always return a shipment and cancel at any time. Even if I never buy another book, the two free books and gifts are mine to keep forever.

154/354 HDN FEP2

Name _____ (PLEASE PRINT) _____

Address _____ Apt. # _____

City _____ State/Prov. _____ Zip/Postal Code _____

Signature (if under 18, a parent or guardian must sign)

Mail to the **Reader Service:**
IN U.S.A.: P.O. Box 1867, Buffalo, NY 14240-1867
IN CANADA: P.O. Box 609, Fort Erie, Ontario L2A 5X3

Not valid for current subscribers to Harlequin American Romance books.

Want to try two free books from another line?
Call 1-800-873-8635 or visit www.ReaderService.com.

* Terms and prices subject to change without notice. Prices do not include applicable taxes. Sales tax applicable in N.Y. Canadian residents will be charged applicable taxes. Offer not valid in Quebec. This offer is limited to one order per household. All orders subject to credit approval. Credit or debit balances in a customer's account(s) may be offset by any other outstanding balance owed by or to the customer. Please allow 4 to 6 weeks for delivery. Offer available while quantities last.

Your Privacy—The Reader Service is committed to protecting your privacy. Our Privacy Policy is available online at www.ReaderService.com or upon request from the Reader Service.

We make a portion of our mailing list available to reputable third parties that offer products we believe may interest you. If you prefer that we not exchange your name with third parties, or if you wish to clarify or modify your communication preferences, please visit us at www.ReaderService.com/consumerschoice or write to us at Reader Service Preference Service, P.O. Box 9062, Buffalo, NY 14269. Include your complete name and address.

HARI1B

*When Forever, Texas's newest deputy, Gabe Rodriguez,
rescues a woman from the scene of an accident, he
encounters a mystery, as well.*

*Here's a sneak peek at A FOREVER CHRISTMAS
by* USA TODAY *bestselling author Marie Ferrarella,
available November 2012
from Harlequin® American Romance®.*

It was still raining. Not nearly as bad as it had been earlier,
but enough to put out what there still was of the fire. Mick
was busy hooking up his tow truck to what was left of the
woman's charred sedan and Alma was getting back into her
Jeep. Neither one of them saw the woman in Gabe's truck
suddenly sit up as he started the vehicle.

"No!"

The single word tore from her lips. There was terror in
her eyes, and she gave every indication that she was going
to jump out of the truck's cab—or at least try to. Surprised,
Gabe quickly grabbed her by the arm with his free hand.

"I wouldn't recommend that," he told her.

The fear in her eyes remained. If anything, it grew even
greater.

"Who are you?" the blonde cried breathlessly. She appeared completely disoriented.

"Gabriel Rodriguez. I'm the guy who pulled you out of
your car and kept you from becoming a piece of charcoal."

Her expression didn't change. It was as if his words
weren't even registering. Nonetheless, Gabe paused, giving
her a minute as he waited for her response.

But the woman said nothing.

"Okay," he coaxed as he drove toward the town of
Forever, "your turn."

The world, both inside the moving vehicle and outside of it, was spinning faster and faster, making it impossible for her to focus on anything. Moreover, she couldn't seem to pull her thoughts together. Couldn't get past the heavy hand of fear that was all but smothering her.

"My turn?" she echoed. What did that mean, her turn? Her turn to do what?

"Yes, your turn," he repeated. "I told you my name. Now you tell me yours."

Her name.

The two words echoed in her brain, encountering only emptiness. Suddenly very weary, she strained hard, searching, waiting for something to come to her.

But nothing did.

The silence stretched out. Finally, just before he repeated his question again, she said in a small voice, hardly above a whisper, "I can't."

Who is this mystery woman?
Find out in A FOREVER CHRISTMAS
by Marie Ferrarella, coming November 2012
from Harlequin® American Romance®.

HAREXP1112

Kathryn Springer

inspires with her tale of a soldier's promise
and his chance for love in

The Soldier's Newfound Family

When he returns to Texas from overseas, U.S. Marine
Carter Wallace makes good on a promise: to tell a fallen
soldier's wife that her husband loved her. But widowed
Savannah Blackmore, pregnant and alone, shares a different
story with Carter—one that tests everything he believes.
Now the marine who never needed anyone suddenly
needs Savannah. Will opening his heart be the
bravest thing he'll ever do?

Available November 2012

www.LoveInspiredBooks.com

LI87776